VAMPIRE ROYALS 2: THE GALA

LEIGH WALKER

CHAPTER 1
BEGIN AGAIN

THERE WAS A KNOCK ON MY DOOR. "MISS? GOOD morning, rise and shine!" My head maid, Evangeline, stuck her pretty face into the room. She took one look at me, and her brow furrowed in surprise. "You're already up?"

I shrugged. "I can't sleep."

She grinned. "Excited about the prince's return?"

My cheeks heated. "No." *Yes.*

"I'll just go and fetch the twins. We'll get your tea ready. Then maybe we can pick out a special dress?"

I looked down at the plain navy frock I'd selected. "Um... Okay?"

She nodded and was gone in an instant, leaving me alone with the tortuous quiet of my room and the rioting thoughts in my brain.

I paced, waiting for her to return with Bria and Bettina, the identical twins who were my other maids. Their pleasant chatter would fill the void. The palace had been quiet, too quiet, these past few days. His Royal Highness, Prince Dallas Black, Crown Prince of the United Settlements, had been gone all week. He'd been traveling with his advisors and guards. Without Dallas, the palace seemed empty and cold.

Evangeline was right. I couldn't wait to see him.

In addition to the prince's absence, fifteen more girls had been cut and sent home from the Pageant, the nationally televised competition in which I was currently a contestant. The Pageant was one-third beauty competition, one-third dating show, and one-third survival boot camp.

I should explain.

Two young women from each settlement had been chosen to participate in the contest. We were "invited," but participation was mandatory. Fifty of us had been brought to the palace, where the king, queen and prince lived. The royal family had conquered the settlements five years ago. We did not say "no" to them.

We didn't dare.

Each girl was given our own room and our own maids. The royal family gave us beautiful clothes to wear. We had our hair and makeup done daily. We attended lessons all day, every day, on etiquette, manners, and all sorts of things.

We were given delicious food to eat. *Oh, the food!* Biscuits and scones and waffles for breakfast. And butter—real butter! Salads, fresh fruits and savory meats for lunch. Succulent roasts, seafood, and potatoes for dinner. Chocolate cake, red velvet cupcakes with cream-cheese frosting and any kind of tart you could imagine for dessert.

My mouth watered just thinking about it, and I wasn't alone. After living on rations for the past five years, all of the contestants were positively giddy about the food.

Our days were filled with meals and lessons, and our every move was filmed for the reality show that followed the competition. Episodes chronicling the girls' lives at the palace were aired weekly, so that the people in the settlements could follow along and root for their favorites.

Thirty girls had already been cut. I was one of remaining twenty, and I didn't know whether to laugh or cry. For those of us left, there was one goal: to win. The champion would become engaged to the dashing, charming prince, Dallas Black. After a royal wedding, she would become the princess of the settlements—and one day, she'd become queen.

But this summary—the same one peddled to the people of the settlements—made the Pageant sound grand and slightly romantic. The truth was quite a bit more complicated than that.

I'd omitted certain pertinent facts, certain deadly, pertinent facts.

The prince was a vampire.

His parents were vampires.

They didn't eat food. They ate...humans.

For instance? My first night at the palace, the queen had bit Eve, the other girl from my settlement, and drained her dry. Now Eve was a vampire.

Since I'd come to the palace, I'd learned that some vampires could control themselves around humans. Others, like the queen, could not. Some vampires could move about in the sunlight. Others would fry. Some vampires, like Eve, had the ability to telepathically speak inside a person's brain. I was still learning all the rules. It was complicated, but if I wanted to stay alive, I'd best pay attention.

The vampire royals had come from the North and conquered the settlements with the Black Guard, their vampire army. Since they'd conquered us, we'd survived on government-supplied rations. We no longer had cell phones, computers or cars. We still had television, though. So the royals could ply us with their propaganda.

My father and older brother had gone off five years ago to fight against them—along with many other human men —and never came home. The human rebel army was still out there. They'd attacked the palace as recently as last week.

On top of all this? The prince had hinted at other threats to the settlements. He'd also mentioned something about other types of vampires and werewolves and...

Stop it, Gwyn.

I rested my forehead against the cool glass of my window, willing the sun to rise higher. During the day, I was busy—busy learning which fork to use at a formal dinner, busy dipping a pen into ink and learning to write polished cursive with flourishes, busy learning how to curtsy without falling on my face.

I liked having my days full because when I was trying to identify the salad fork, I could hide from the truth: I'd fallen for the prince—the *vampire* prince.

This was also complicated by certain pertinent facts, including, but not limited to, the nineteen other girls living at the palace. Based on the way they all sighed and fluttered their lashes every time the prince was near, they'd also fallen for him and wanted to marry him.

And then there was the whole, *you know*, vampire thing. And the fact that Dallas had told me I smelled quite delicious, which I think meant he wanted to bite me. My thoughts kept wandering, wondering what else he might like to do to me...

The door burst open, and my maids swept in. Evangeline, tall and blonde, led the way. Close on her heels were the twins, Bria and Bettina, their coffee-colored skin flushed and their almond-shaped eyes glittering with excitement.

But Bria stopped in her tracks. She took one look at me and frowned. She headed straight for my wardrobe.

"What's the matter?" I asked.

"I think you know," she scolded. Her ponytail swung in her wake, highlighting the blue ribbon she always wore so people could tell her apart from her sister. "There is no way you're wearing *that* wretched dress today. Who wears navy-blue cotton to a royal reunion?"

I sighed, looking down and smoothing my modest dress. "There's no reunion planned. I don't even know if I'll see the prince today."

"Of course you will. You're his favorite! Everyone says so." Bria tore through my closet, dismissing a dozen dresses until she found one she liked. She pulled out a gauzy blue gown that looked suspiciously low cut.

"I don't know about that one."

"Just try it!" Bria handed it to me and unzipped the dress I was wearing without further ado.

I'd learned there was no use in arguing.

I stepped into the new gown, and Bria pulled it up. Bria and her sister, Bettina, ogled me, clapping their hands and squealing in unison.

"Just gorgeous!"

"You are stunning, my lady!"

Evangeline finished pouring my tea and had a look. "Oh, miss, it's very becoming. Come and see."

They ushered me to the full-length mirror, and my jaw dropped when I saw my reflection. The dress was gorgeous but very revealing. The top was low-cut and skintight. It showed off my pale skin and curves. The skirt skimmed me, blue chiffon billowing in soft waves to the floor.

"It's lovely, but..." I tried to pull up the bodice to no avail. "Isn't there more to it somewhere?"

"No, that's everything." Bria grinned. "I adore it."

I cleared my throat. "I'm not sure that it's, ah, appropriate."

"But the prince will love it," Bria whined. "And that *Tamara's* worn things much more brazen." She sniffed.

Tamara was one of the other remaining contestants from a prominent family from Settlement 11. Some of the other girls whispered that she was favored to win the competition. Tall, with a statuesque build and long raven hair, she had no problem flaunting her many enviable assets —much to the chagrin of my maids and many of the other girls.

"Tamara and I have different...er, styles." I coughed. The fact was, Tamara would strut around the palace in a string bikini morning, noon and night if it were allowed. "I think it's a good thing."

Evangeline laughed behind her hand, and Bria went back to the wardrobe. She selected a pretty tangerine-colored frock with a more modest neckline. "What about this one?" She sounded dejected.

"I love that dress. It's perfect. As for this one"—I fingered the layers of the skirt—"I'll save it for a special occasion. You're right about the prince. I think he'd be partial to this."

Mollified, Bria helped me change. Then she forced me into a chair and started brushing the snarls out of my long, thick hair. "I'm going to make your hair shine. The prince will go wild."

"We don't need to make him wild, exactly," I said through gritted teeth, as she worked out a particularly difficult snarl. A wild vampire might be dangerous.

But the thought of Dallas being excited to see me kicked up my heart rate. I forced my mind to quiet as my cheeks heated. *Ridiculous.* Just the talk of his return to the palace had me needing to fan myself.

Bria mumbled something under her breath, which sounded suspiciously like, "*Oh, yes we do.*"

I pretended to be above the conversation and ignored her, simultaneously and secretly willing my hormones to calm down.

Bettina set a heavy crate full of makeup on a nearby table and grinned at me. "Don't let my sister get under your skin. She wants you to shine, is all." She took out a tub of some sparkly gold substance and dipped a poufy makeup brush into it.

She dabbed it onto my nose. "Speaking of shining..."

I closed my eyes and let them finish with my hair and makeup. Back home, my normal beauty routine consisted of brushing my teeth and throwing my hair up into a messy bun. The twins shuddered whenever I told them that, so I gleefully reminded them frequently.

Bria worked through all the snarls then fluffed and smoothed my hair. Bettina slathered on what seemed like ten layers of makeup while Evangeline tidied and dusted the room, humming under her breath.

"Ladies." I opened my eyes. "If I haven't said it lately, I want you to know I appreciate how well you take care of me." I missed my mother and younger siblings terribly, but the maids had become my second family. They fussed over me and scolded me like I was one of their own.

Bettina swatted me on the nose with the poufy brush. "It's our pleasure, miss. We love having you and the other girls at the palace. The competition's brought a whole new life to this place."

"And you thank us often." Evangeline smiled at me kindly then added another log to the fire.

Bria finished with my hair then leaned down to grin at me. "And there's no one we'd rather serve. You're *our* favorite too, you know."

There was a knock at the door. Evangeline answered it. "Yes?"

"His Royal Highness, Prince Dallas Black, Crown Prince of the United Settlements, is here," the guard announced.

The four of us looked at each other, shocked. The twins sprang into action, putting away the makeup and brushes in a frenzy. Bria gave my hair one last insistent fluff.

"Yes, of course. Just a moment." Evangeline eyed the room then, declaring it fit for the prince, swept to the side and stood at attention. Bria winked at me as she and Bettina joined her in their customary positions at her side.

I stood and smoothed my dress. My hands shook. *He's here.* Nervous excitement thrummed through me, but fear lurked beneath.

I was afraid. *Afraid of just how much I've missed him.*

In a few short weeks, the prince had become awfully important to me, and I meant "awful" literally. It *was* awful thinking about him all day, every day, tossing and turning at night, wondering if he was okay, wondering if he was thinking about me... It was both awful and wonderful to be so consumed.

But oh, my God, I'd gone soft over him.

I pushed the rampant thoughts to the side as Dallas strode into the room, looking as if he'd come in from a long ride. His cheeks were flushed, and his hair was a bit wild. He smelled of the outdoors.

He smiled at my maids and greeted each of them. "Evangeline. Bria. Bettina." His kindness and attention to the staff was just one of the things I admired about him.

My maids curtsied then righted themselves, looking as if *they* now needed to fan themselves.

The prince turned his dark-eyed gaze to me, and I sucked in a deep breath. It had only been a few days, but I was still struck by how tall and handsome he was. My eyes raked over his pale skin, square jaw, and broad shoulders.

I exhaled and shakily curtsied, praying I didn't faint. It wouldn't be the first time. "Your Highness."

He bowed. "My lady."

"I wasn't expecting you back so early."

Dallas favored me with a large smile, his dimple springing forth in all its glory. "I'm afraid I couldn't bear to stay away much longer."

I thought I heard the twins sigh. Evangeline gave them each a filthy look then quickly composed her features.

"How was your trip? Everything went well, I hope?"

His smile disappeared. "It went as well as I could expect. How has the palace been?"

"Fine. Everything's been running smoothly. Tariq's got us learning about fork tines." Tariq was the royal emissary. He was largely in charge of the Pageant—a fact he never let any of us forget.

Dallas chuckled, relaxing again. "Ah, Tariq and his forks."

The prince took a step toward me, and my heart pounded. I desperately hoped he couldn't see it flutter against the thin material of my dress. "I missed you, Gwyneth."

I took a steadying breath. "I missed you too, Dallas."

A guard stepped through the door. "Your Highness, I've just had word. They're ready for you."

Dallas nodded then turned back to me, his gaze burning. "I'm sorry, but I have to go. I need to meet with my court and update them with news from my travels."

I tried not to appear crestfallen that he was already leaving. "Of course. Thank you for coming to see me."

He grinned. "My pleasure."

I took a quick step toward him. "Are you sure everything's all right?" Rebels had recently attacked the palace, and I worried that they planned more onslaughts.

He reached for my hand and squeezed it. "It will be. And you have my word that I'll keep you and the others safe. We'll talk more of it later."

I wasn't worried about my safety, and I had about a million more questions, but the guards waited outside the door. "Okay."

He released me. "I'll come see you as soon as I can."

With another bow, the prince was gone, his cape trailing after him.

And I just stood there, heart thudding in his wake.

CHAPTER 2
A MONTAGE I'D LOVE TO FORGET

EVEN THOUGH ANOTHER FIFTEEN GIRLS HAD BEEN CUT and sent home, you'd never know it from the high-pitched ruckus coming from the common room.

"The prince is back! I saw the guard riding in with the banners this morning!" gushed one young woman to her friend.

"I heard he's going to resume the one-on-one dates tonight. I hope he picks me!" squealed another.

"It's been soooo boring here without the prince. I've resorted to double espressos." Another girl tossed her thick, blonde ponytail over her shoulder then held up her shaking hand.

Her friend giggled, but the girl frowned. "I think I need to tone it down a bit. I don't want to frighten him!"

I wanted to remind her that the prince was a vampire—making him eminently more frightening than a highly-caffeinated human—but instead, I made a beeline for the table occupied by my closest contestant-friend, Shaye Iman.

She wore a blush-pink dress, her tawny curls tumbling past her shoulders. Her makeup shimmered, pink and perfect, making her copper-hued skin sparkle. As usual, she was dazzling.

Shaye grinned at me as I grabbed a biscuit. "So I'm guessing you heard... Prince Charming is back in town. It's all everyone's talking about."

I shoveled some of the biscuit into my mouth and nodded. I didn't want to tell her I'd already seen him. I wasn't sure if it would hurt her feelings. Shaye liked the prince, too, a fact I was still trying to come to terms with.

"Oh, Gwyn knows all about that." Bosom bursting with untold gossip, Tamara plopped into the seat next to me. She leaned conspiratorially toward Shaye. "My maids told me the prince went to her room this morning."

I swallowed hard as Shaye's jaw dropped. I glared at Tamara. "Your maids should learn to mind their own business."

Tamara arched a perfectly sculpted eyebrow at me then arranged her emerald-green gown. "Already acting like you're the boss, eh?"

"You shut your mouth—"

"Ladies." Tariq suddenly appeared, beaming down at us. As usual, the royal emissary was perfectly put together. His dark hair was ruthlessly slicked back, and he wore a deep-purple ceremonial uniform. His expensive cologne wafted over our table. "Everything quite all right?"

I cleared my throat. "Yes, Your Royal Emissary."

"Everything's fine." Tamara fluttered her eyelashes at him. "Just a little morning girl talk."

He turned to Shaye. "Miss Iman?"

"We're good." But she blushed beneath her makeup, and I wondered just how much the news of Dallas visiting me bothered her.

"Most excellent." Tariq's eyes glittered. "I have something quite special to share with you all this morning—the latest episodes of the Pageant. We're airing two back-to-back installments tonight. The viewers are going to be beside themselves with excitement."

He leaned down, nodding to Shaye and Tamara. "Both of your one-on-one dates are featured. They are to die for."

He strutted off, and a heavy silence settled over our table. Tamara beamed, Shaye tore at her napkin, and I stuffed another biscuit into my mouth.

⚜

PLATINUM-HAIRED MIRA KINNEY STOOD IN FRONT OF the large flat screen, looking lovely and elegant in a nubby-fabric skirt suit. She was the government-sanctioned television personality narrating and hosting the televised version of the Pageant. She and her crew were living at the palace, filming us around the clock.

Mira Kinney was a prime example of how my life had been turned upside-down since entering the contest. She was a vampire, but she lived and worked among us girls as if it were no big deal. Before I'd come to the palace, I hadn't even known vampires existed.

But I'd learned that some vampires, like Mira and the prince, could coexist peacefully with humans when they wanted to. When they didn't want to, like when Dallas had fought the human rebels, it was an entirely different story.

Other vampires, like the queen, had self-control issues around humans. Since the queen had ravaged Eve, they'd kept her away from us, thank God.

"We've gotten great feedback about the first episode." Mira broke my reverie. "Based on early polls, it appears that close to ninety percent of the population tuned into the premiere. That's a staggering number. The approval ratings for the government have skyrocketed. I want to thank everyone for their hard work and contribution to the show's success."

Her sharp, blue-eyed gaze sought out mine. "I'd like to specially recognize Miss West, who stayed calm under pressure. She had the first one-on-one date with the prince, and she handled it flawlessly."

The other girls clapped politely, and I smiled, but then I saw Tamara glaring. She looked as if she might scratch my eyes out. I hastily scooted away from her.

"We're airing two episodes of the competition tonight," Mira continued. "We're looking to capitalize on the viewers' excitement. With only four weeks of the competition remaining, we're going to be increasing the number of broadcasts. We want the people of the settlements to feel as if they're taking this journey *with* you. We want them to feel everything you're feeling."

One of the other girls raised her hand. "What's going to happen over the next four weeks? Is everyone going to get a one-on-one date with the prince?"

Several other girls murmured in the crowd, echoing her question.

Tariq stepped out of the shadows. "I'll explain everything about the coming weeks in my lecture later this morning, after Mira's finished with her presentation."

Mira nodded. "I want you all to watch these episodes closely, then we're going to review each of them, section by section." She smiled at us, revealing her perfect, even white teeth. "You can learn a lot by watching these two young ladies. Both of them wowed on their one-on-one dates."

Tamara tossed her hair, and Shaye slunk into her seat.

"What's the matter?" I whispered.

Shaye just bit her lip and shook her head, looking worried.

Tamara's episode aired first.

I settled in to watch the opening sequence. The royal crest was the initial image, accompanied by the United Settlements's anthem. Then came footage of the King and Queen. They stood side by side, aloof and regal.

Mira Kinney said, in a voice-over, "Introducing His Royal Majesty, King Reginald Black, Crown King of the United Royal Settlements and his wife, Her Royal Majesty, Queen Serena Black, Crown Queen of the United Royal Settlements. The King and Queen are thrilled to welcome the Pageant contestants to the palace."

King Black was tall, muscular, and handsome, with gray hair and a trim, white beard. The Queen was stunning, tall and lean, with sapphire-blue eyes, a high forehead, and a long, graceful neck. She was beautiful, but I still shivered with dread when I saw her.

The familiar brief, propagandized version of how the royals had come to power in the settlements followed. They were portrayed as saviors, coming down from the north to rescue us from crime and poverty. The images on the screen showed the royal family—the king, the queen, and the prince—waving to adoring onlookers at a midnight parade. Then there was a group of young women wearing gowns, eagerly smiling as a long line of paparazzi took pictures of them. The last image was of a young woman kneeling, a crown being placed on her head.

Next came the prince. The film showed him riding a white steed, wind whipping through his hair. He had his own segment, during which he declared himself ready for love, commitment, and marriage. As usual, many of the girls sighed with longing as we watched him.

Next, each of the remaining contestants was shown. Our names and settlement numbers were broadcast across the screen.

"Miss Gwyneth West, Settlement Four."

I barely recognized myself with my hair and makeup done and dressed in an elegant red gown.

The first scene showed Tamara with her maids, getting ready in the morning. The sun shone brightly in her room, illuminating the dark waves of her raven hair. Her skin positively glistened, and her bosom heaved as her maids zipped her into a tight scarlet gown then ushered her to the full-length mirror.

She smiled at her reflection, and why shouldn't she? She looked gorgeous. She looked like a princess.

I bit the inside of my cheek so I didn't groan out loud as the program continued. Tamara flirted, flounced, and stuck her chest out at the prince every chance she got.

In one scene, she "accidentally" bumped into him, squishing her enviable assets directly into his chest and his direct line of vision.

I grimaced as I watched Dallas smile at her. Still, I knew him well enough to see that he didn't really seem interested in Tamara. His body language was stiff, formal. He smiled at her without warmth, a fact that seemed largely lost on her. She openly gloated as we watched the episode, tossing her hair and grinning at anyone who looked her way.

Tamara's episode ended with footage of her and the prince on the front steps of the palace—the part of their date I'd interrupted. Of course, my intrusion was edited out. The final images were of Dallas with his arm around Tamara, his hand securely fastened to her lower back. She looked adoringly up at him as he smiled for the cameras.

She fist-pumped as the credits rolled. "That was epic!"

Insipid cow, I thought.

I composed my features. "You looked very pretty."

She shrugged, beaming. "Thanks."

Shaye leaned forward. "It was a great episode. The camera loves you."

Tamara crossed her legs. "It does, doesn't it?"

I rolled my eyes, and Shaye silently giggled.

But she stopped abruptly as the next episode began. Shaye slunk down in her seat, as if she wished she could disappear.

"Sit up and watch, silly!" I hiss-whispered.

She scootched up a bit, eyes wide and never leaving the screen. I wondered what had my friend so tense. She'd told me that the prince had kissed her but that it had been quick and chaste. As I watched her slink back down in her chair, I wondered if she'd been minimizing it.

"Shaye Iman is from Settlement Twenty-Four, as far west as the settlements go," Mira Kinney said in a voice-over. "Her life back home is humble."

The image panned to what I assumed was the town Shaye came from in Settlement 24. It was little more than a village. The center consisted of several small, shabby-looking houses and a run-down store. The streets were muddy. Children in dirty clothes played in the square, and dogs roamed around in a pack.

It was dark, but I knew Shaye's cheeks were flaming red. "But nobility comes from within. Miss Iman's adjusted extraordinarily well to palace life. Easily one of the most graceful, humble and kind contestants, she's adored by the royals and staff alike."

The next images showed Shaye smiling kindly at the kitchen staff, helping the gardeners wrangle an unruly rose bush, and bowing elegantly before the prince. It also showed her at our breakfast table, laughing and chatting with Tamara and me as we feasted on raspberry scones. Extremely pretty in person, Shaye was unequivocally stunning on screen.

Next was an image of Shaye walking arm-in-arm with the prince around the reflecting pools in the garden. Mira's voice-over continued. "Miss Iman was instrumental in advocating for generous stipends for the Pageant's contestants. Of course, the royal family fell in love with the idea, and each contestant will leave the palace with a healthy cash prize to thank their families for their service to the settlements."

Shaye kept her arms wrapped tightly around herself as she watched. Tamara sat ramrod straight, a grim, resigned look on her face. Because even Tamara would have to admit it—not only was she gorgeous, Shaye's kindness and quiet dignity came across clearly in the episode. The settlers were going to go wild for her. She was a Cinderella story in the making, and she would make a magnificent princess.

A princess for the people.

"As she was chosen early in the competition for a one-on-one date, the prince also clearly appreciates Miss Iman," Mira's voiceover narrated.

The scene changed to the night of Dallas and Shaye's date. Shaye wore a lovely, blush-pink dress, similar in color to the one she wore today. But in the episode, the gown had a full, layered-tulle bottom. It gave the dress a floating, magical effect, as if Shaye might fly up and sprinkle fairy-dust on the prince. And given the way he kept staring, the prince was certainly enraptured by her.

Now it was my turn for flaming-red cheeks. I wasn't entirely sure I could watch this part.

The crew had filmed them during their date. They had dinner in a formal dining room I'd never seen before. There were candles everywhere and an enormous bouquet of roses in the middle of the table. Dallas wore his dark-gray ceremonial uniform, his hair tousled and wild.

He sipped wine while he watched Shaye eat, his gaze never leaving her face.

"What are you staring at?" Shaye blushed.

Dallas smiled in response, his dimple flashing. "You are lovely," he said, simply.

They stared at each other.

I wanted to run from the room, screaming, but I couldn't move. I couldn't tear my eyes away from the screen.

After their dinner, Dallas led Shaye to the grand foyer. They made a beautiful couple. His skin was icy pale, but hers was a rich, warm copper. They complemented each other perfectly, light and dark, each shimmering in the candlelight from the massive chandelier.

"It was nice to spend time with you, Shaye." Dallas loomed over her. "You are...easy to get along with."

Shaye had told me he'd said this, but hearing it like this was a punch to the gut.

"Thank you, Your Highness. I had a lovely evening." Shaye curtsied and went to take her leave, but Dallas gently stopped her. He bent down and brushed his lips against hers.

He pulled back. "Good night, miss."

She curtsied again, a little wobbly this time. "Your Highness."

My heart twisted, and I squeezed the arms of my chair. Tears pricked my eyes. But I refused to cry, steadying myself with deep breaths as the credits rolled. By the time the lights came up, I'd plastered a huge smile across my face.

I hugged Shaye, hard.

"What's that for?" The question came out muffled. I might have squeezed her too forcefully.

"That was a triumph." I pulled back, beaming at my friend. "You were wonderful."

Shaye's eyes were wide, unsure. "T-Thank you."

"You did very well," Tamara sniffed, butting in. "I still don't think what he said was that romantic, but it's a start, I guess."

Shaye's face went scarlet. She nodded her assent. "You're probably r-right."

"Don't be such a jealous cow, Tamara," I snapped.

Suddenly, several other girls descended on us, peppering Shaye with congratulations and questions about the prince. I sat back and watched my friend answer them, polite and kind as always.

I still felt sick, as if someone had sucker-punched me in the stomach.

Tamara leaned closer, narrowing her eyes at me. "As for being a jealous cow?" She kept her voice low. "It takes one to know one."

"Shut *up*, Tamara."

But I knew in my heart she was right.

CHAPTER 3
WHAT FOUR WEEKS OF HELL
LOOK LIKE

MIRA KINNEY DISSECTED EVERY SCENE IN BOTH OF THE episodes, talking about posture, eye contact, and camera angles, but I didn't listen to a word.

All I could think of was Dallas. And Shaye. And Dallas *with* Shaye.

I knew him well enough to know that he wasn't interested in Tamara. But I could see, quite clearly, that he was taken with Shaye.

Why would he do this to me? Why had he lied and said he only had eyes for me?

Why would he come see me first thing this morning?

Why had he made me hope?

The episode dissection ended, and Mira dismissed us. My head throbbed as I headed to the lecture hall, where Tariq was giving our next lesson. Both Shaye and Tamara were uncharacteristically silent, which suited me fine.

"Are you all right?" Shaye asked, as we took seats in the hall.

"Of course." I fake-smiled so hard my face hurt.

"I told you he kissed me." Shaye sounded defensive.

I nodded quickly. "I know you did."

Tamara rolled her eyes, but I ignored her, grateful that Tariq was already at the front of the room, ready to speak.

"Ladies, first of all, congratulations. You are the final twenty contestants. Nicely done." He clapped, and we joined him. "Now, as I stated previously, there are four weeks remaining in the competition. I have several announcements about that."

He waited as murmurs broke through the group then continued. "No one will be cut for the next four weeks. Each of you will have a one-on-one date with the prince. For those of you who haven't done that yet, you are the priority. All first dates will consist of a formal dinner, as they have to this point."

The girls whispered until Tariq cleared his throat. "That being said, his royal highness will also be spending individual time with the girls he's already had first dates with. Second dates will be given to whomever the prince requests, and they can occur at any time."

More chatter erupted, and Tariq held up his hands. "Ladies, please." The room quieted down again. "Second dates will be more adventurous, you might say, than first dates. If you are chosen for a second date, you can expect to do an activity with the prince. These might include horseback riding, hiking, archery, or dancing."

Several of the girls *oohed* and *aahed*.

Tariq smiled, pleased with the response. "The point of a first date is to see if you and the prince can have a conversation and enjoy a meal together."

Except Dallas can't eat anything, I thought meanly. *So he'll just gaze at you longingly and flash his traitorous, duplicitous dimple. Because apparently, he does that to all the girls!*

"The point of a second date is to see if you can enjoy an activity together and whether or not you have shared interests. I must stress that these second dates are very, very important. The prince takes the competition seriously. He is looking to find his life partner, and he wants to see who he most enjoys spending time with."

I snorted then quickly disguised it as a cough.

"At the end of the four weeks, the palace will host a royal gala." Tariq beamed as excited cries and chatter broke throughout the audience. "Each of you will be dressed in a gown befitting the company of the royal family. At the end of the night, the final four contestants will be announced."

He paced the front of the room. "We are going to be filming you every second over the next few weeks. As Mira said, we want the audience to take this journey with you. We want them to feel what you feel—your triumph, your hope, your heartbreak."

Tariq eyed us, letting that sink in. "The next episodes of the Pageant are going to get very personal. We want to involve the audience as much as possible so they're invested in the outcome. It's good for all of the settlements. I had high expectations for this competition, and it's working out better than I'd hoped. People want a princess they can believe in, who they can relate to. They need to see you as normal girls, risking your hearts to find true love. I need all of you to do your best, to commit to this process even more so, and to give it all you've got. The reward is a husband and a kingdom."

The room was silent for a moment. Then Tamara raised her hand. "What happens after the finalists are announced?"

She asked the question confidently, as if she had already had a vested interest in the answer.

Tariq nodded. "Each of the final four girls will have one last week with the royal family. The prince will visit each of their settlements and meet each girl's family. At the end of that week, the winner of the Pageant will be announced, and plans for the royal wedding will begin in earnest."

Tariq didn't bother to try to quiet us after that. The room erupted with talk, each girl discussing their individual position and what the coming weeks would bring.

"Well, this should be...fun," I said haltingly.

Shaye smiled tightly. "Absolutely."

"I can't wait for my second date." Tamara inspected her nails. "I am going to show the prince that I'm *very* good company."

Shaye frowned. "What's that supposed to mean?"

"Nothing, Miss Innocent." Tamara shrugged. "It just means that he'll enjoy his time with me. I'll make sure of it."

The way she said it made me want to go take a shower.

"Do you think we can go, now?" I didn't want to hear any more about Tamara's questionable plans for the prince. I simply wanted to go to my room and be alone. And maybe pretend Dallas was my pillow and then punch the living daylights out of it.

"Ladies, you are dismissed until the afternoon sessions." Tariq bowed.

I hastily took my leave, hustling into the hallway, full steam ahead. I planned to have my way with that pillow—

"Gwyneth. Why do you look as if you're about to blow your stack?" Dallas suddenly stood in front of me, an amused look on his face.

I clenched my fists together. "Oh, you...*you*..."

He arched an eyebrow. "This a 'me' issue? Do tell."

I put my hands on my hips, either too angry to speak or just winding up—I wasn't sure.

Sensing an oncoming public tirade, Dallas gently took me by the arm. He led me through a door and outside onto the eastern lawn. Closing the door behind us, he made sure no one was near. "What did I do now?"

"You kissed Shaye!" I roared.

He arched an eyebrow. "I already told you about that, and if I recall correctly, so did she."

"I just saw the episode," I spluttered, "and you were tripping all over yourself, following her around!"

He waited to see if I'd go on. When I didn't, he cocked his head at me. "If you'll remember, I had my date with Shaye right after you'd said that my people were—now wait, let's see if I can remember it all correctly, you did rather go on—ah, yes. 'Mind controllers who would slaughter all of humanity in an instant.' Isn't that what you said?"

I lifted my chin. "I explained myself. I told you that I struggled after I saw the rebel attack."

"And I told *you* that I barely kissed her," Dallas said. "And that at the time, I didn't know you cared."

I took a deep breath, trying to calm down. "You seemed...into her. It looked real."

"Shaye was kind to me. I appreciated it."

"It looked like you did more than appreciate it."

"She was *nice* to me when you were not."

I scoffed. "You'd just slaughtered a hundred humans and burned them in a funeral pyre on your lawn. 'Nice' wasn't available, Your Worship!"

Dallas's eyes flashed. "I'm not human, but I still have feelings."

"Oh, fine." I haughtily pulled myself to my full height. "You go and have all the feelings you want!"

I hustled back inside, and Dallas cursed, hot on my trail. "You are being a child, Gwyneth—"

"Ah, I've been looking for you." Tariq blocked my escape down the hall.

I peered around him, desperate for escape. *For the love of all things holy, get out of my way!*

The prince caught up to me, and we briefly glared at each other. Then we turned our attention to Tariq, who watched us with thinly veiled interest.

"Yes, Tariq?" I tried to keep my voice neutral. "What can I do for you?"

"I was going to tell you about tomorrow, but I guess His Highness has informed you of your special plans together."

"Um..." I swallowed hard.

"I haven't told her." Dallas sounded grim.

"Ah, well then." Tariq bowed toward me. "You have the honor of having a second date with the prince tomorrow. I'll have your maids instructed—they need to pack you. You'll be gone all morning."

"I... Uh..."

"Get plenty of sleep tonight. The camera crew will be following you. They'll be filming every precious second." Tariq beamed then bowed again. "Your Highness. Miss West."

I didn't miss his smirk as he turned on his heel and swept off.

That just left Dallas and me.

"Are you finished berating me then running away like a coward?" he asked.

"I think I'm done. And I'm not a coward! I'm simply...

pissed." I cleared my throat, cheeks heating. "Your Highness."

"Ah. Simply pissed, is it? Sounds easy enough to manage. I'll leave you to it." I might've imagined it, but his eyes sparkled.

I coughed. "Thanks."

"Well then...see you tomorrow." I caught a flash of the prince's dimple before he strode off.

At least someone was amused.

I just stood there, fists still clenched, not knowing whether to laugh or cry. But then I remembered my pillow.

Suddenly feeling better, I stalked off to punish it.

CHAPTER 4
ONLY HUMAN

AFTER SOME TIME MUTTERING TO MYSELF, BEATING UP ON the Dallas Pillow and stomping about my room, I went to see my friend Eve. A newly minted vampire, she'd only recently been cleared for limited unsupervised contact with humans. I was allowed to go to her chambers every other day for ten minutes. It wasn't much, but at least we could talk.

I kept to myself as I headed to her chambers, noticing that the increased security at the palace remained. Since the rebels had attacked, more guards had been posted both inside and outside on the grounds. The guards' weapons were visible, strapped across their chests. I hoped that all of this was an unnecessary precaution.

I tried not to think about the guards recently killed inside the palace. Benjamin Vale, the prisoner who'd tricked me into letting him out of his cell, had shot them. One of the guards was the young man who'd come to my home and escorted me to the palace. I tried not to think about him, but his face often flashed in my head. I sighed, aching with regret. I needed to be careful, much more careful, about who I trusted from here on out.

When I arrived, Eve was practicing combat moves. She'd cleared a space in her room for training. Dressed in a tunic and pants, she twirled a stick in her hands, landing in a defensive pose. Her strawberry-blond curls bounced.

"You really look like a badass," I said.

She turned her blazing aqua gaze to me and grinned. "I don't just look like one. Watch this."

She twirled the stick around in a complicated maneuver that made me dizzy. She ended with the stick poised sharply above the ground, ready to pierce her invisible enemy. "See? I'm learning! I'm a real-deal badass."

"But what do you need the stick for? Can't you just...you know?" I flashed my teeth at her and hissed.

Her shoulders shook with silent laughter. "You seriously suck at that. No pun intended."

I giggled. "Oh, fine, tease me. But really, why the combat training?"

"Since I'm immortal now and I have all of eternity to practice, I'm thinking I should up my ass-kicking game a bit. Might as well make it look pretty. Bring some art to it."

I added "immortality" to my ever-growing list of Things About Vampires to Ponder.

Eve put the stick against the wall. "I'm surprised to see you today, actually. I heard His Royal Brooding-ness was back in town."

I nodded. "He's back, all right."

"So why the long face?"

I sighed. "I'd tell you, but you'll just laugh."

She plopped into an overstuffed chair and motioned for me to do the same. "Try me."

"It's silly, and I know it." I sank down across from her. "We watched a couple of the Pageant episodes this morning. He had one-on-one dates with two of the other girls."

Eve frowned. "It's a dating competition. Of course, he's going to have dates with the other girls."

"I know." I sighed. "But he...he kissed one of the other girls."

"Hasn't he kissed you?"

"No, he hasn't."

Eve raised her eyebrows. "Probably because he's been too busy saving you—"

"Or..." I interrupted.

"*Or* you were too busy being difficult."

I blushed furiously. "That's not the point. The point is, he made me feel like I was the only one he cared about. But he lied, Eve. He looked at this other girl like she was special —really special. And the thing is, I know her. She's a great girl. She *is* really special." I groaned.

"He has to kiss the other girls, especially the 'really special' ones." Eve rolled her eyes. "He has a part to play. He can't just herd girls from every settlement to the palace and then politely say, 'Oh, sorry! My bad, I already made my choice! Gwyn's so great. She has pretty hair and a nice bum and is posh and all that, so you've all got to go home now. Game over! And by the way, please tell your parents not to rise up and join the rebels!'"

I giggled, but she stared me down. "It's not funny, Gwyn. There's a lot at stake."

I sighed. Both she and the prince had hinted about threats to the settlements. "Can you tell me more? Because I know for a fact Dallas won't."

"That's because he's trying to protect you." Eve's

unusual eyes burned with intensity. Ever since she'd been
turned, her eyes had glowed. "You know, I give him a hard
time, but you're brutal. All he wants is to keep you safe."

"I know. He's protected me more than once. And it's not
just that... I care about him."

"But that's good, right?"

"I don't know because I don't know if I can stand this—
watching him with the others. It makes me doubt everything, like I don't know what's real." I sighed. "I guess I'm
just a defective human."

Eve's face softened. "Human news flash: the prince likes
you. *Really* likes you. Any idiot can see that—no offense."

She chuckled while I frowned.

"But he still has a role to play. The Pageant's a game,
Gwyn, a contest. There are a lot of players and moving
pieces. It's not all moonlight and roses. He has his parents
to please, the settlements to keep in line, the peace to
keep... It's political."

"I understand that. I don't like it, but I understand it." I
frowned again.

"But?"

"But what happens... What if I fall in love with him?
And he chooses someone else?"

Eve nodded. "You've got to decide how brave you can
bear to be—and if you think he's worth it."

I nodded at my friend, but I was anxious to change the
subject. "What about you? You seem like you're getting on
well. I'm so impressed."

Eve bounced her knee, energy radiating off of her. She
was probably anxious to get back to her stick. "I love being
a vampire."

I sat forward, shocked. "You *what?*"

She shrugged, smiling. "I love it. I feel so strong. I have so much energy, and everything's so clear—it's like my senses are on overdrive all the time."

"Tell me more."

Eve sprang up and paced, stretching her limbs. She tossed her hair. "I dunno. It's like I could a climb a mountain then fight a lion then sprint for miles then battle someone or other then do jumping jacks. And never need to sleep."

"But do you? Sleep, I mean?"

"A little." Eve frowned. "It's more like resting, really. I stay in my bed for an hour or so and close myself down. But I don't really sleep."

"What about eating?" Dallas had mentioned that Eve had rejected donated blood. She wanted to hunt instead.

"Now that you mention it, I *am* starving." We looked at each other for a moment, and my heart stopped. She giggled. "I don't want to eat you, Gwyn. I mean, you smell fantastic and all, but... Ew."

"Dallas said you wouldn't drink the donated blood."

She rolled her eyes. "His Superiority-Complex finally got me to start drinking it. It's fine."

Fascinated, I had more questions. "Is the queen still visiting you at night?" After savaging Eve, the queen had become maternal toward her, coming to her room in the middle of the night and stroking her hair.

Eve nodded. "She asked me to dine with them soon. I think she wants to be friends or something, of all the odd things I'd never expect."

"Huh. How do you feel about it? About being here, after everything?"

In her old life, Eve had hated the vampires. She'd called

them *filthy bloodsuckers*, which is what got her bit in the first place.

She went and stood by the window, staring out at the grounds. "I think it was fate. I think I was meant to come here, to be turned."

She was quiet for a minute. Just when I thought she wouldn't say more, she continued. "My mother's dead. I had no one left at home, nothing. I was invited here for the opportunity of a lifetime, but I didn't see it that way." She looked back at me. "You remember, don't you?"

I nodded. She'd been very vocal about her distaste for the royals, their guard, and the Pageant.

"At first, I thought I was being punished. I thought the queen turned me to be cruel. But now I see it differently. Being a vampire is an opportunity."

"What do you mean?"

"I was prejudiced. I hated them, hated all of their kind. But now I live among them, and I'm forced to see as they see, feel as they feel. And I know now I was wrong. There were plenty of humans who treated me worse back in my old life. You can be a monster no matter who you are. It's a choice. The royals punished me, but they were fair. They've treated me with kindness ever since."

"So you're not...unhappy?"

"Not at all. I know it was for a reason. I was weak before, and now I'm strong. I'm going to use that to help others—all others. Human and vampire."

There was a knock on the door, and one of the guards stuck his face in. "I'm afraid time's up, my ladies."

"It was nice to see you." I stood and squeezed her hand. "I'll come again soon."

"Keep me posted. And try to remember the big picture."

"Since when did you get so philosophical?"

She grabbed her stick and twirled it. "Since my human life ended and I've been forced to contemplate my immortality. It sort of does that to a girl—makes you reflective."

"Keep me posted on that."

I hustled down the hallway. Head still brimming with the conversation with my friend, I was anxious to get back to my chamber and be alone with my thoughts. I closed my door and paced my room, occasionally looking at the fire.

I was happy for Eve. I was also shocked at how quickly she'd adjusted to her new life, but I shouldn't have been. From the moment I'd met her, she'd been sharply aware. My friend was too smart to fool herself for long. She was making the best of what had happened, and I admired her for it.

I was glad to hear of the royal family's continuing kind treatment of her. From the beginning, Dallas had made a point of taking her under his wing, and had promised to train her.

Dallas. My thoughts kept circling him. Even after the cringe-worthy experience of watching him and Shaye in the video, I was still excited for our date tomorrow. I didn't even bother lying to myself about that. I just wanted to be near him, even if I was still pissed.

I thought about what Eve had said. She was right. It was a dating competition, and I'd known that from the beginning. She also had a point about the roles we had to play. Dallas had his, and I had mine.

I cared for Dallas—deeply. *Too deeply.* I was already in over my head.

So what would I do if I couldn't swim back to the surface?

I'd never been in love before. If the heart was a muscle, mine hadn't been trained to handle the ups and downs of this competition. Truth be told, I wanted to run and hide. I didn't know if I could bear the coming weeks. But I couldn't be a coward. I had a family back home—a starving family—to take care of. For the past five years, we'd barely hung on, trading all of our possessions and family heirlooms for firewood and food. The Pageant was our one shot at a better life. The generous stipend would save us. I had to hang on at least for that.

And if I won...what was it Tariq had said? The prize was a husband and a kingdom. I could save my own family and the future generations.

So I was going to stay. I would fight to win.

Still, I was afraid of the depths of my feelings for Dallas. I could feel it—that swift under-current that threatened to pull me under. So I would stay, but I would guard my heart against the prince.

No matter what it wanted, or how it ached.

CHAPTER 5

A CHANGE OF SCENERY

"GOOD MORNING, MISS. HERE'S YOUR TEA." EVANGELINE bustled about the room, setting down the tea tray and opening the curtains.

I glowered at the sun streaming through the windows. "What time is it?"

"Six a.m., miss. You have a long morning ahead of you, and the prince wants to get an early start. The twins and I will be back with your outfit. We've already packed a bag for you. The staff will have it downstairs. The camera crew was granted permission to come and film you getting ready, so you might want to get up before they barge in here."

"Ugh." I sank back underneath the covers. "Who gave them permission?"

"Tariq."

"Of course he did." Tariq was probably gleefully looking forward to my date with the prince after he'd caught us glowering at each other yesterday. Drama was good for ratings.

With everything else on my mind, I'd forgotten that

they'd be filming our date—I needed to work on my fake smile—stat.

"Do you have any idea what I'm doing today?"

Evangeline grinned. "I'm not sure of the particulars, but I know it involves a riding suit."

I sat up straight. "We're going riding?"

Her eyes sparkled. "Your guess is as good as mine, and I think it's a pretty good guess. I'll be back in a moment with the twins."

She closed the door, and I hopped out of bed, suddenly energized. I hadn't ridden in years. The idea of being outdoors with a horse beneath me and the wind in my hair—oh, it was magnificent. I gulped some tea and slathered extra butter on my toast. I peered out the window, watching the sunrise. A gorgeous day, a perfect day—even if His Duplicitous Dimple-ness was riding beside me, and the whole thing was being filmed for public consumption.

The twins bustled in, excited smiles on their faces. I waited for their normal ribbing, but when the film crew squeezed in behind them, I understood. We had our game faces on. They sent me to the bathroom and put me into a steel-gray riding outfit, fitted and flattering. The cameras filmed us as they hauled me back out and plopped me into a chair. Bria braided my hair with extra care, and Bettina insisted on seven layers of makeup, even though I'd be outside all day.

"Are you ready, miss?" Evangeline asked, when the final round of powder had been applied to my nose.

"Yes. I am."

Nervous excitement thrilled through me as I descended the stairs in my riding boots. The camera crew stayed close behind, and I was relieved to be in the boots, not the high heels they usually made us parade around in.

Dallas waited in the grand foyer. I sucked in a deep breath when I saw him. As tall as ever, his black riding boots were polished to a deep, lustrous sheen. His tight-fitting riding suit accentuated his broad, muscled form.

I grabbed onto the railing, lest I fall and trip anyway, even in flats.

He bowed deeply when I reached the bottom of the stairs. "My lady. Thank you for accepting my invitation."

I arched an eyebrow but then, remembering the cameras, curtsied appropriately. "Your Highness."

He held out his arm for me, and I took it. His scent wafted over me, making my mouth water, making me dizzy.

He was like a contact high. *Get a grip, Gwyn!*

But Dallas was the only thing to hold onto, so I did, grasping his forearm so I didn't collapse into a puddle at his feet. *Stupid, traitorous hormones.* They didn't seem to hold a grudge like the rest of me.

"I thought we'd go riding," Dallas said, as we went through the front doors. "I understand you used to ride at the Academy. I was hoping this was something we could enjoy doing together."

I nodded encouragingly. "I'm thrilled. I haven't ridden in years."

"Then I hope you'll like this." We swept down the stairs and were greeted by the sight of two of the most beautiful white mares I'd ever seen.

I stopped in my tracks. "Oh, Dallas. They're gorgeous."

He leaned in closer so no one could hear us. "I'm working hard to earn your forgiveness."

Before I could respond, he released me. "Now, I picked

Maeve for you." He indicated the slightly smaller horse. "She's amazing and gentle but has real power. Are you comfortable going out now, or do you want to re-acquaint yourself with a saddle a bit first?"

I stroked the mare's mane, basking in her beauty. "No, I'm ready," I said, a bit breathlessly.

Dallas smiled widely. "Excellent. I thought I'd show you around the grounds and take you to one of my favorite spots. Have you had breakfast?"

"Yes." I couldn't tear my eyes from Maeve.

"I took the liberty of having a generous amount of food packed, anyway. We'll ride for a bit and then stop to eat." He motioned behind the horses, where numerous guards waited, each with a horse of their own. "We won't be alone, of course. My guard and the cameras are following, but I expect we can have a bit of a head start." He climbed up and settled onto his saddle, and I was momentarily blindsided by the sight of him, so handsome and regal on his horse.

He beamed down at me. "Gwyneth? Are you ready?"

"Yes, of course." I climbed up on Maeve and relished every sensation, the stirrups around my feet, the reins in my hands, and the feel of the horse's powerful body beneath mine.

Dallas clicked his reins and cantered off. Maeve and I followed close behind. We went slowly at first, getting acquainted with each other. I thrilled as the castle grew smaller behind us and acres of open, rolling lawn stretched out in front me. I itched to let the horse take off, to run free at top speed.

Dallas looked back over his shoulder. "Are you good?"

"Yes!"

He grinned, and his horse shot forward.

I urged Maeve into a gallop, and we went after him. The rest of the world fell away as the wind rushed past me, whipping my braid.

I came even with Dallas, and he grinned again, the sun sparkling on his white, white skin.

And then I saw it for the first time—he looked happy. Truly happy. His smile reached all the way to his eyes.

We rode off, leaving the castle and everything else behind.

❧

I DIDN'T KNOW HOW MUCH TIME HAD PASSED, BUT WE rode for miles, finally meeting the trees. Dallas slowed his horse, coming to a stop before a dirt road that cut through the woods. "There's something up ahead I want to show you. The others are close behind—I'll have them bring some food and drink when they finally catch up."

"That's very kind." We cantered next to each other, and I inhaled a deep breath of fresh air. It was late winter, but it was milder here than back at home. The sun warmed my face.

I looked around the wood filled with white pine trees. "It's so beautiful."

"I agree." Dallas kept his gaze firmly on me. "Riding becomes you."

"Thank you. It was my favorite thing to do before the... Before." Before the war, I'd ridden every day. Once the Blacks had taken over, they'd confiscated all the horses.

"My family took the horses so the rebels couldn't utilize them," Dallas said, as if he'd read my thoughts. "We brought them here. Many of our horses had been killed in battle or died of disease up north."

"Oh." I didn't know what to say.

"Did you own your own horse?"

"No. I had a favorite at our stable, though. Ginger. She was a sorrel, just as sweet and beautiful as can be. She had a lovely red coat." I smiled, remembering my old friend. "I brought her sugar cubes and carrots. She was basically my BFF."

He cocked an eyebrow. "I'm sorry? What's a 'BFF?'"

"A Best Friend Forever. Do you have one?"

Dallas considered that. "Hmm. Well, my friend Lucas is pretty close. I think I've mentioned him before. And of course, there's Austin, my younger brother, although I have half a mind to throttle him at the moment."

I almost choked. "You have a younger brother? You only mentioned your sister…"

His sister was dead. That's all I knew.

"Ah yes, I have a younger brother. He's up north, still. Refuses to leave our old home and come down here and assume his responsibilities."

"Why?"

Dallas's face grew stormy. "If you ask him, he's got plenty of reasons. But I know he just likes having the old castle to himself, even if the rest of the land's filthy with werewolves and all other manner of rot."

When my face contorted with confusion, Dallas remembered himself. "Ah, here we are."

"Did you just mention werewolves again?"

He smiled tightly. "The cameras are coming. Let's save that for later, shall we?"

I nodded stupidly. But I wasn't sure there was later enough for the topic of *werewolves*.

Dallas stopped his horse and jumped off, motioning for me to do the same.

I came beside him then noticed a small path that cut through the woods.

He reached for me. "Come with me, Gwyn. I've something *much* more exciting to show you than a filthy werewolf."

CHAPTER 6
I NEED EVERY WAKING HOUR
WITH YOU

I HADN'T REALIZED I'D BEEN HOLDING MY BREATH UNTIL we walked down the path and come to a clearing, bordered by a large, stone ledge.

I peered around. "This is it?"

"Nothing's going to jump out at you, I promise."

"You really aren't going to show me a werewolf?" I asked, half joking. "Or a troll, or...maybe a gnome?"

He chuckled. "Trolls are only from bedtime stories."

"So what about the—"

"Come. I just want to show you." He took my hand. "There's a beautiful view from up here." Dallas started up the path, pulling me gently behind him. "It gets a little tricky, so watch your step." We hiked around the corner, and I gasped when we got to the top. Acres of green grass stretched before us, followed by the blue waters of an enormous lake.

"This is beautiful."

Dallas sat down on the edge and patted the spot next to him.

I sat down, and he surprised me with a friendly hug. He put his big arm around me, squeezing gently before releasing me. "I'm so glad we got to do this today."

"I am as well."

Dallas looked out at the lake. "I wasn't sure how it was going to go, after your little fit yesterday."

"I beg your pardon." I bristled, feeling my face turn red. "It was *not* a fit."

"Was so." He laughed at me.

I clenched my fists, about to launch into a tirade, but then I remembered myself. I had to learn to play the game.

Must. Calm. Down. Must. Not. Yell.

"You're right, Your Highness. I guess I *did* have a bit of a...fit." I struggled to get the word out.

He stopped laughing and frowned. "Why are you agreeing with me? That's not like you."

I cleared my throat. "I'm trying to be more open-minded."

"No," he said, no longer laughing. "You're trying to let me win my point. Why?"

I looked at him and quickly looked away. "I don't want to be difficult."

"That's not like you."

"I'm not that bad, you know. I can be easy to get along with, too." The words, the ones he'd used to describe Shaye, burned my tongue.

"You're right—I don't think you're bad at all. But you aren't easy to get along with. And I don't want you to be."

I looked at him sharply.

"The reason I enjoy your company is because you're usually honest with me. That's refreshing. I don't have a lot of people in my life who are truthful about what they think and feel." He ran a hand through his hair, making it stand up in unruly spikes.

I didn't say anything. I couldn't.

Dallas's eyes darkened. "But if you're just playing a game and telling me what I want to hear—I'm sorry, but I don't have time for that. I'm already up to my eyeballs in that sort of nonsense."

"That's not what I'm doing." I sighed. "Well, all right, that's what I was doing."

"My dearest Gwyneth, I do believe you're lying to me by agreeing with me again."

"I am *not*, Your Lordship," I huffed. "Not right now. I was for a bit. For a second."

I looked at him, but he stared straight ahead. "I'm sorry. I'm trying to...protect myself. By agreeing with you, which I'm sure makes absolutely no sense."

"No, I understand. I've been on the receiving end of that sort of thinking my whole life. People tell me what I want to hear, so they can get what they want."

"It's not like that..."

Ugh. I sat there, not knowing what to say next. He knew me better than I'd guessed—even my brief attempt at playing the game had caught his sharp notice.

He didn't say anything for another minute. Finally, he tapped my chin, bringing my face closer to his. "Don't do that to me again. Please. Don't tell me what it is you think I want to hear. It makes me feel as if you're another stranger to be tolerated."

Intensity crackled between us as I held his stare. "I won't. I sort of sucked at it, in case you couldn't tell."

He chuckled but then turned serious again. "Promise me, Gwyneth."

"I promise. I'll always tell you what I think, even if you don't want to hear it. And I bet you won't want to hear most of it."

The camera crew and soldiers came around the corner, and he released me. I wished we were still alone. The fresh air and the riding had revived me, and the conversation with Dallas had been...real. Honest.

I'd been kidding myself that I could shield myself from my feelings for him. All my ugly thoughts of the prince with Shaye were slipping away, already almost forgotten.

The guards brought up a basket, set it gingerly behind us, then bowed at Dallas. He opened it, taking out a tin, some butter, and a knife. He put everything between us. He pulled the lid off and I moaned. "Oh, you got biscuits."

"I know you like them." His eyes sparkled as he took one out, buttered it, and handed it to me. Then he pulled out a bottle of rosé and a wine opener.

"Wine with breakfast?"

"Don't judge me." He smirked. "The producers told me I have to do something while my dates eat, so it doesn't look awkward."

"Ah. So you look...occupied."

The people in the settlements didn't know that the royal family were vampires. There were rumors, of course. The royals' oddly pale skin and foreign manner had people questioning. And when they'd come down from the North to conquer the settlements, the Black Guard only attacked at night.

Now that I'd gotten to know about vampires, I understood that some of them, like Dallas, Eve, and Mira Kinney, were perfectly capable of coming out during the day. Others, like the queen, avoided the sun at all costs.

None of them ate, though. They only ate...drank... blood. And wine.

So the prince's wine was a prop, something for him to hold onto in order to avoid looking awkward while his human dates ate or drank. They hadn't addressed the prince's vampirism in the show, yet. Dallas had mentioned that he wanted to, but I didn't know what his father had to say about that. I wondered when and if they would. I couldn't imagine what my mother would say. Probably something akin to *deal with it* or another one of her all-time favorites, *suck it up*.

Oh, the irony.

Dallas poured himself some rosé and motioned at the crew. "You should get a shot of the lake. It'll be nice for the viewers to see how pretty it is, here. And then you may film us for ten more minutes. But when we continue our ride, Miss West and I would like some privacy."

"Of course, Your Majesty." The camera crew bowed, immediately setting up to take a shot of the view.

"Must be nice to have people follow your orders."

He shrugged. "It has its benefits, but it also has draw-backs, which is why I expect my brother's still hiding up north. He doesn't want to deal with the drawbacks."

"Do you mean—"

"Let's talk of it later." Dallas poured me a glass of water. "Now, tell me about when you were younger and all about your BFF, the lovely Ginger."

AFTER OUR BREAK, WE CONTINUED OUR RIDE ACROSS THE

grounds. The guards and the camera crew kept a respectful distance. We slowed our pace, able to finally talk in peace.

"While I have you, I need to get something off my chest."

My heart thudded in my own chest. "Yes?"

"I'm sorry about yesterday," Dallas said. "I wanted to come to you last night, but Eve warned me not to."

"Eve? What on earth did she say?"

He gave me a quick look. "That you'd been to see her. She made it sound very human—something like you needed 'space' and 'time to process.'"

I shook my head. "Eve is very wise, all of a sudden."

"The transformation can do that to you. It pushes a lot of things that can clutter a human's mind to the side."

I bristled. "Oh, like what?"

"Like worrying about whether people like you or not."

I lifted my chin. "You don't worry about that?" With his title, that broad chest and all that hair, he probably never had to.

"No, I do. Sometimes." He gave me a pointed look. "But enough about that—I was apologizing to you. I think you missed it."

"I didn't miss it." I sighed. "And I'm sorry, too. I didn't react well to watching the episode."

Dallas frowned.

"But you don't need to apologize," I said quickly. "You didn't do anything wrong. You have a job to do, a role to play, girls to romance."

"I appreciate that you understand. But you know that there's...more to come." He looked miserable. "I cannot reject all the other girls out of turn. They've come here and left their families, hoping for a better life. At the very least, they deserve a fair chance."

I nodded. "I understand. Eve and I talked about this very thing yesterday—how I needed to remember 'the bigger picture.'"

He raked a hand through his hair. "But how are you going to handle it? Every time you're forced to watch an episode, you're going to doubt me."

"Doubt you how?"

He frowned again, as if this was enough of an answer.

I scratched the horse behind the ears. "When I feel bad, I will simply have to remember this day, and my dear Maeve." She whinnied beneath me. "I shall remember the kindness you showed me."

He relaxed a bit. "Today's been my pleasure. There's nothing I'd rather do. And you're really very pleasant company when you aren't lying to me or biting my head off." He chuckled.

Before I could argue, we rounded a corner, and the castle came back into view. Dallas visibly stiffened.

"One more thing, Gwyneth. I haven't forgotten about your family. I had what I thought was a lead on the whereabouts of your father and Balkyn, but the trail was cold. Nothing's been confirmed."

Dallas had promised to find out if my father and brother, who'd joined the rebel army and been missing for five years, were alive or dead.

I clutched the reins. "What did you hear? Are they alive or dead?"

"I don't know. I didn't want to bring it up, but I also didn't want you to think I'd forgotten."

I stopped Maeve. "Please. Anything you can tell me—

even if it turns out to be false—I want to hear it. I haven't had any news of them since they left, aside from the lies Benjamin Vale told me." I shuddered, thinking of the dead rebel and how he'd tricked me into believing he knew where my brother was.

Dallas stopped his horse and stared at the castle, his face stormy. "I don't want to give you false hope."

My heart rate quickened. "So you heard they're still alive."

He nodded. "But I don't know if it's true. I don't want you to be completely crushed if it isn't."

"If they're dead, I'm going to be completely crushed anyway." I waited until his gaze met mine. "Thank you."

"As soon as I hear something, I'll come to you." He nodded, and we took off at a trot.

"Is there any news of the rebels?" I hoped my inquiry wouldn't upset him.

The muscle in his jaw jumped. "Nothing good, I'm afraid. That's part of the reason I had to travel. They've been very active in making threats."

"That must be difficult."

"It's more dangerous than it is difficult."

I guided Maeve along the path, unsure of what to say. The rebels were humans. My father and brother had gone off to fight with them. Until I'd come to the palace, I'd considered them my people.

But whatever my connection to the rebels, I still cared about the prince's well being. "Are you safe? Are you worried about another attack?"

"My safety's the last thing you need to be worried about. And as for another attack, I have pledged to keep you safe."

"I'm not worried about me."

His nostrils flared. "You don't need to be. That's my job." Dallas was a wee bit overprotective.

"I'm sorry to have brought it up, but of course, it's on my mind after what happened." A rebel army had attacked the palace a few weeks ago. The royals had killed most of them and taken a few prisoners—one of whom was the treacherous Benjamin Vale, who Dallas had drained dry after he'd tried to escape.

"I know you're in a difficult position. Caught between two worlds, I suppose." Dallas's gaze raked over me. "Yours and mine."

"There is only one world. And I don't want anyone—on either side—to be hurt. I don't think that's a difficult position, do you?"

He looked thoughtful. "No. Not when you put it that way, Gwyneth. It doesn't seem difficult at all."

CHAPTER 7

MY FRIENDS THEY ARE SO BEAUTIFUL

"ONE LAST STOP BEFORE WE HAVE TO GO BACK." DALLAS guided his horse to the left of the castle.

"Where are we going?"

"You'll see." He picked up speed, and I followed, sad that we were back so soon. Hours had passed. I was likely needed at curtsying practice, but given the choice, I would've kept riding Maeve until the moon came out.

We rounded the corner and came to a large, white barn and sprawling stable. "I want to show you where your new friend Maeve lives, in case you ever want to come and see her."

"Would I be able to do that?"

"Absolutely. I'll have it arranged with Tariq that you're able to come out here every day, and I'll try to take you riding again when I can. I'm afraid it's not safe for you to go out on your own."

"Because of the rebels?"

Dallas arched an eyebrow. "Or the garden gnomes," he said, clearly teasing.

"Ha-ha." I came even with him.

"Why're you frowning like that?"

"Are there really such things as garden gnomes?"

"Hmm. Well, they don't all live in gardens, I suppose. Only the civilized ones do that."

My jaw dropped. "There are uncivilized gnomes?"

"I'm going to let you keep guessing about that." His eyes twinkled. "Here we are."

We stopped at the stable, and two groomsmen came out, taking the reins for us. They were both human. When I'd first come to the palace, I'd been shocked by how many civilians worked for the royal family. They co-existed peacefully. I'd mostly gotten used to it, but every once in a while, it gave me a jolt.

Vampires and humans, living together in peace. It was certainly not something I'd ever expected.

We climbed off the horses and I stroked Maeve's mane. "Thank you for a wonderful ride," I told her.

She whinnied in response.

Dallas beamed at me as the men led the horses to their stalls. "It appears you have a new friend."

I couldn't wipe the smile from my face. "She's amazing."

Dallas held out his hand for me. "Let me introduce you to the rest of the horses and show you around."

"Thank you."

"It's my pleasure, Gwyneth."

I DIDN'T WANT TO LEAVE THE STABLES—EVER—BUT WE had to get back. Dallas and I held hands as we walked. The camera crew trailed us, and I briefly wondered what the other girls would say when this episode aired.

They weren't going to be happy. *But speaking of their happiness…*

"Your—Dallas, I was wondering something."

"Nice save." He smiled at me. "And yes?"

"Would it be possible for the other girls to come out to the stable, too? I know they'd love it. Everyone was so excited when we got to the castle and saw all the horses."

He stopped walking. "That's very kind of you to include them."

"I told you I'm not all bad."

He brought my hands up to his lips and kissed them.

My heart did a somersault as our eyes locked.

He leaned forward, and I lifted my face, but there was suddenly a cough directly behind us.

"Your Highness?"

Dallas turned to the guard, his face twisting with annoyance. "Oh, for the love of all things holy, your timing's horrible."

"I'm so sorry to interrupt." The guard coughed again. "It's the king, Your Majesty. He's requested you immediately."

The prince smoothed his features. "I'm coming."

"Thank you. I'll let His Majesty know. And my apologies about the timing." The guard's eyes crinkled in a mixture of regret and humor.

He strode off before we could all be embarrassed together.

Dallas sighed. "I'm sorry about that."

I smiled up at him. "Duty calls. I understand—and no, I'm not just being agreeable."

"Good. Nicely done." Dallas leaned down and gave me a brief kiss on the cheek—brief, but it still made my whole body tingle.

I sighed as he pulled away. "Thank you for a wonderful morning."

"I enjoyed it more than you know." He looked toward the castle and cursed. "I have to go."

I nodded.

"One last thing." He leaned back down next to me and inhaled.

"Are you *sniffing* me?"

He pulled back, dimple on full display. "Yes. You are delectable, Gwyneth, if I do say so myself."

My cheeks heated. "That's a compliment, right?"

He tucked a hair behind my ear. "The highest kind, where I come from."

He turned to the guards and I realized that they, and the entire camera crew, were watching us, transfixed.

"Please see Miss West safely to her lesson," he instructed the guards. Then he turned to me and bowed. "My lady. It's been a pleasure."

I sighed as I watched him stride away, hoping that the crew wouldn't catch my fangirling on film.

❧

"OH, DEAR LORD." NOW I KNEW WHY MY MAIDS HAD left out running tights, a tank top and athletic shoes for me to change into.

The "lesson" that Tariq had planned was nothing more than a glorified workout. All the girls had on athletic clothes, too, and he was running them through a circuit. Kettle bells, jump ropes, and mini-bands littered the floor.

Every girl I passed had a red, sweating face and frizzy hair.

The girl with the thick, blond ponytail and the caffeine jitters nodded as I walked by. "He's trying to kill us, I swear." She did another bicep curl with a weight and grimaced. "He's had us at this all morning."

"Why?"

"He wants us to look good for the cameras." She put the barbell on the floor, wiped her hand on her tank top, and held it out for me to shake. "I'm Blake, by the way. Settlement Fifteen."

"I'm Gwyneth, Settlement Four."

Blake grinned at me, and I noticed for the first time how pretty she was. "Oh, I know who you are. Everyone does."

"They do?"

"Of course! You're the girl the prince can't stay away from." She didn't say it in a mean way.

"Is that what people think?"

She shrugged. "That's what they *say*. You never know what they're actually thinking."

I laughed. "True."

"Did you have a second date this morning?"

I nodded.

"And?"

"And it was lovely."

Blake grinned. "Good for you. I'm totally rooting for you."

"You are? Aren't you rooting for yourself?"

"Sure, but the prince doesn't seem too interested in me."

She picked up the barbell and started on another set. "I'm just psyched to still be here. I haven't had this much food in five years."

I laughed, warming to Blake. I admired her honesty. "Me too."

She winked at me. "And heads up—I'm pretty sure Tamara's prepped to grill you. She's been on the warpath about your date all morning."

My heart sank. "Great. Thanks for letting me know."

"Anytime."

I headed for the back corner, where Shaye was rather listlessly jumping rope and Tamara was aggressively doing squats, while watching her form—or maybe her amazing glutes—in the mirror.

"Hey." I picked up a mini-band and turned it over, wondering the heck to do with it.

"How'd it go?" Shaye practically tripped over her jump rope and stopped. "Geez, I guess I can't jump and talk at the same time."

"Tell us everything," Tamara commanded, dropping into another deep squat. "We need to be prepared for when it's our turn."

I took the mini-band and wrapped it around my fingers, making a cat's cradle. Then I flexed my fingers, as if this constituted working out.

"We went riding."

"Horses?" Tamara snapped.

"We didn't ride unicycles, silly."

She frowned. "Details, please."

"It was nice. The horses were gorgeous."

"Those aren't the details I'm looking for. Did he kiss you?"

I narrowed my eyes. "No."

Relief flitted across Shaye's face so quickly I might have imagined it.

"It was a morning date," she said supportively, recovering quickly. "It doesn't mean anything that he didn't kiss you."

"Says the girl who's already been kissed." Tamara arched an eyebrow then turned her attention back to me. "I don't understand why he keeps sniffing about when he hasn't even kissed you yet."

"He kissed my cheek," I mumbled, face reddening.

"You and your ever-loving cheek. I might die of boredom." Tamara whipped her ponytail around as Tariq approached us.

I wasn't usually happy to see the royal emissary, but anything that interrupted Tamara was welcome relief.

"Ladies." He bowed then turned his attention to me. "How was your morning? The crew reported they were very happy with the footage. I can't wait to review it."

"We had a wonderful time."

Tamara made a gagging noise, but I ignored her. "In fact, there's something I'd like to speak to you about."

His eyes sparkled with interest. Tariq might be the biggest gossip of them all. "Yes?"

"Dallas—His Highness—offered to let me visit the stables daily, so that I might see the horses and enjoy some fresh air. But we'd like all the contestants to be able to participate. I know he was going to talk to you about it, but I just wanted to ask. Is that something you'd be willing to consider?"

"His Highness agreed to open stable privileges for all the girls?"

"Yes."

"Then of course, I'm amenable to it." He stroked his chin, considering. "It will be good to share that sort of kindness with the viewers. I think it's an excellent idea. Thank you for bringing this to my attention, Gwyneth."

He bowed again and left. He must've been pleased because he didn't even yell at me for not exercising.

Both Tamara and Shaye were staring at me. "What?"

Tamara snorted. "'*We'd* like all the contestants to participate'?"

My face reddened again. "The prince and I talked about it this morning. I didn't mean—"

"You didn't mean to sound like a superior, snotty bitch?"

"Whoa." I extricated my fingers from the mini-band and tossed it to the ground. "You did *not* just call me that."

Tamara puffed out her sports-bra-clad chest. "Did so."

I took a step closer. "If anyone's a superior, snotty—"

"Hey." Shaye stepped between us. "Knock it off, you two."

Tariq came hustling back, distracted. "By the way, I forgot to mention: Tamara, you have a second date with the prince tomorrow. Details to follow!"

He paused, noting the two of us glaring at each other. "Is there a problem, ladies?"

"Not anymore, Tariq." Tamara relaxed, beaming at the news of being chosen for a second date. "I was just about to show the girls how to do a proper squat."

Tariq shrugged one shoulder at her. "You know you're the best at that."

She snapped her fingers. "That's the truth."

It took every ounce of my willpower not to throttle the insipid cow.

"Ladies." Tariq bowed and was off, again.

"Well, that's better." Tamara tossed her ponytail and stalked back to her position near the mirror. She resumed her relentless squatting, looking as if she were dropping into a tiny, tiny stool. "I can't wait to be alone with the prince again."

"You're a prat, Tamara."

She winked at me. "At least you won't die of boredom when you hear how *my* date goes. I'll be sure to keep it interesting."

And I'll be sure to smack that smug look off your face.

"Fine." I rolled my shoulders back and grabbed a jump rope, as if I couldn't care less. "May the best woman win."

"Well that would be Shaye," Tamara quipped. "And lord knows *she's* not going to win."

Shaye put her hands on her hips. "I beg your pardon!"

"Face it, you're too nice." Tamara dropped into another squat. "But I'm not."

I continued to jump rope, issuing a litany of curses under my breath. These included, but were not limited to, *prat, cow,* and *entitled-Settlement-11 squat-loving douche-nozzle.*

But I just kept jumping and kept the insults to myself.

The prince had shown me a kindness today. I would not let Tamara undo my happiness.

I would not let her win.

CHAPTER 8
GOT NOTHING ON YOU

I HAD A LETTER FROM MY MOTHER THE NEXT MORNING.

Dear Gwyneth,
I watched the next two episodes. Those girls have nothing on you,
although I will say the one from Settlement 24 has a good story,
coming from such a poor home. It's probably fake, a ploy by her
family to win favor.
Why didn't we think of that?
The other girl, the one with the long black hair, was positively
intolerable. Such a fake. She's good-looking, though, I have to give
her that. She'll land on her feet. Mark my word.
I still think your date was the best. The prince might've kissed that
other girl, but he didn't look at either of them the way he looked at
you. Have faith, my dear.
We're counting on you.
Which brings me to the reason for this letter. I don't want you to
worry because you need to take care of yourself, but Winnie's been
quite ill. She's had a high fever. I had Dr. Northman come to see her,
but he doesn't have any supplies left. I'm not sure what we'll do

next. I'm watching her nonstop. Please pray for her, Gwyneth?
Send a funny note with news of the prince. That would cheer
her up.
I'll write again soon.
Keep up the good work.
Love,
Mom

I folded the letter up and went down to breakfast in a fog, worried about my sister.

"Gwyneth, a word." I looked up to find Dallas waiting for me in the hall.

I nodded, absentmindedly following him into the library. He closed the door behind us.

He raked a hand through his hair. "This is awkward."

I looked around, still distracted. "It is?"

"Yes." He sighed.

"Is this about Tamara?" I asked, trying to make sense of what he was saying. "I know you have a date with her. But honestly? If you fall in love with her—and all that hair and those glutes and her attitude—we clearly aren't meant for each other, anyway. So I won't be mad, just disappointed in your taste."

He laughed or coughed; I couldn't be sure. "Good to see that you're back to being your honest self, but that's not what I'm talking about. It's about the letter."

"The letter from my mother?"

"Yes, which is why this is awkward. I know Tariq informed you all, but palace security reads and reviews all incoming and outgoing correspondence."

"Yes." I was aware of the policy.

"I'd told the staff that I had a...special interest...in your letters." Clearly embarrassed, his words tumbled out on top of each other.

"Dallas, are you blushing?" I didn't know vampires could.

"No." He swiped his big hand through his hair. "Maybe. Anyway, it doesn't matter. First thing during my early morning meeting, I was alerted to the fact that your sister had taken ill. I took the liberty of sending some of our medical staff to care for her. I wanted you to know. I hope you won't be upset."

"Why would I be upset?"

"Because I meddled like an old lady. I read your letter without your knowledge. And then without even asking you, I contacted your family and sent my staff to your home." He stood stock still, fists clenched, waiting to be judged.

I ran to him.

I threw my arms around his neck and buried my face in his broad chest. "Thank you." The words came out muffled. "Thank you, thank you, *thank you*."

He tentatively put his hands on my back. "You're welcome. I thought you might be angry with me for violating your privacy."

"I couldn't care less." I pulled back, wiping my eyes. "My brother and sister mean everything to me—that's what I care about. I was so upset when I read the letter. I didn't know what to do."

"The doctor I sent is fantastic. She'll take good care of your sister." Dallas nodded. "I'll let you know how she is as soon as I have word."

"Thank you, Dallas. I will never be able to say that

enough." I hugged him again, and he gently hugged me back, putting his face against my hair.

"I have to go." He reluctantly released me.

I felt cold without him. "I know. You have a date with *Tamara*."

His face twisted. "If you weren't angry at me about reading the letter, you're sure to be mad at me about that."

I straightened myself. "No, I understand you have things to do. You're a diplomat, after all."

"With the monarchy, I'm actually more of an autocrat, I'm afraid. But yes, things to do..."

I lifted my chin. "In any event, date you must. I'll be fine. Tariq has promised us time in the stables today, so I'll have Maeve to comfort me while you're off on your...adventure."

"Thank you for understanding." His gaze burned into me.

I gave him one last look as I headed to the door. "You're helping me keep my family together. It's the least I can do."

"Gwyneth."

"Yes?"

"I'll be thinking of you."

My heart did another tricky somersault. "And I, you."

Blushing furiously, I headed down the hall.

"DO YOU KNOW WHAT THEY'RE DOING ON THEIR DATE?" Shaye carefully brushed her mare's black coat.

"I don't. If Tamara has her way, it'll be skinny-dipping."

Shaye shuddered. "She wouldn't."

I scoffed as I brushed Maeve's coat to a glossy sheen. "Of course she would!"

Maeve whinnied, and I clucked my tongue, soothing her. "There, there, we all know Tamara's a prat. But the prince has to date her. Yes he does."

Shaye giggled. "You're handling this better than I thought. You two seemed like you were going to come to blows yesterday."

"I shouldn't let her get under my skin, but *ugh*. She's the master."

"She's a pro, all right."

I started working carefully on Maeve's mane. "She didn't mean what she said yesterday about you. About not winning."

Shaye shrugged. "Yes, she did."

"She's wrong, though. I think being nice is an advantage. It beats being a self-obsessed showoff."

"I don't know. She's the one on the second date." Shaye wrinkled her nose. "We'll see if I even get one."

"Of course you will." No matter what, Shaye was my friend. I wanted her to do well, even if it was directly opposed to my own interests.

Shaye patted her horse. "It's so nice that we get to come out here. The horses are beautiful."

I nodded. "It's a good change of pace, I think. Better than tripping around in heels and counting fork tines."

"Not to eavesdrop, but speaking of forks." Blake stuck her head into our stall. "I heard we're having turkey tonight."

"A roast turkey?"

Blake nodded, eyes shining. "The kitchen maids told

me. There's going to be cornbread stuffing and cranberry relish—all the trimmings."

"Oh, I can't wait." I clutched my stomach. "I'll have to skip cheese and crackers this afternoon, so I can have seconds."

"Or thirds." Shaye smiled.

"And dessert." Blake grinned.

"Come in here and help us, will you?" I grabbed a rake to spread fresh hay around the stall.

"My pleasure." Blake grabbed a rake and jumped right in.

"Have you had a date with the prince yet?" Shaye asked her.

"Nah. He just doesn't seem into me. I don't know why he kept me around."

"Um, maybe because you're tall and gorgeous?" Shaye eyed Blake, who was indeed almost six-feet tall, with long, willowy limbs. Her thick, golden hair cascaded down her back.

"Thanks." Blake shrugged. "I dunno. He doesn't ever seem to be looking in my direction, but I'm so excited I wasn't cut. I'm in no rush to go home."

"What's Fifteen like?" I asked.

She shrugged again, but her easygoing manner seemed to dissipate a bit. "It's pretty depressing, actually. We've been struggling since the war. I have three siblings, and my dad's been sick. He's gone downhill in the past couple of years. I think it's because of the stress and honestly, poor nutrition."

Shaye frowned as she spread hay. "I'm so sorry."

"It's all right. I still have my dad. I know a lot of the girls here don't."

"Like both of us." I pointed to Shaye and me. "Our fathers and older brothers went to fight and never came back."

Blake shook her head. "That's terrible."

"But maybe they're still alive." I raked with renewed vigor. "You never know."

"Right." Blake smiled at me. "I hope so. Anyway, anybody want to bet on Tamara's date with the prince? I have three chocolate croissants that say she either kisses him or somehow gets him to carry her at some point. Anyone?"

"Hmm. I'll see your three chocolate croissants, and I'll raise you a raspberry scone. And I don't think he'll kiss her." He wouldn't. I couldn't picture it.

I thought for a moment. "She might have him carry her, though. He would do that if she needed help. Good call."

"I like raspberry scones, so I'll take the bet on the kissing." Blake shrugged. "Works for me. We have a deal."

I chuckled and spread more hay. Although I knew I would also want to smack her, part of me couldn't wait to hear how Tamara's date went.

CHAPTER 9
A BIT OF A STIFF

TAMARA SWEPT INTO THE COMMON ROOM AT DINNER, head held high, and I inspected her carefully for any signs of kissing. But of course, she simply looked flawless, not a smudge of makeup out of place. I hoped to be the proud owner of three plump chocolate croissants before the night was over.

She ignored the other girls' curious stares. She would make them wait to hear about her time with the prince, whipping them into a frenzy. She came directly to our table, settling in next to Shaye. "Ladies, I have an announcement."

Blake leaned over from her nearby table, all the better to eavesdrop.

"The prince kissed me."

I cursed under my breath while Blake pumped her fist.

"So now Shaye and I are obviously holding the top two spots in this competition." Tamara smiled sweetly at Shaye. "I'm in first, of course."

Shaye tried not to choke on her turkey. "Of course."

"Tell us everything," I encouraged.

I needed details. The prince was going to get a bloody earful from me before I never spoke to him again.

Tamara shrugged. "Well to start with, he's quite boring."

Shaye almost choked again, but I kept my face neutral. I had to hear this.

"We played chess, of all things. I was hoping for something a little more athletic, so I could flaunt my...skills...but he wanted to play chess so we did. Because he's the prince."

Tamara stabbed a forkful of almond green beans. "I let him win the first time, of course—because again, *he's the prince*. But then his eyes glazed over, and he started to look a bit put out, so I decided to make it more interesting."

"What did you do?" I asked.

"I made him a bet."

"Ooh, do tell. I love a good bet." I winked at Blake.

Tamara gave me a funny look. "Since when were you talking to me again, anyway?"

"Since I decided not to kick your ass yesterday, and I'm sort of stuck with you for the next four weeks. Plus, I'm nosy," I reminded her.

"Whatever. And for the record, I would've kicked *your* ass." She shrugged, but unable to keep herself from bragging about her date, continued. "I bet him that if I lost, I had to do whatever he wanted, even if it was playing basketball. Or even playing more chess. But if I won, he had to do whatever I wanted."

Shaye arched her eyebrows, as if to ask, *Skinny dipping?*

Tamara tossed her hair over her shoulder. "So I'm actually quite good at chess, but he didn't know that because I'd fumbled through our first game on purpose. So I let him think he was winning for the first half, but then I snuck back and beat him quite handily."

"And what did you choose as your prize?" Shaye asked.

Tamara glowed with triumph. "I asked him to kiss me. That's what I wanted."

I cursed again, wondering if I really had to give up that scone. He'd kissed her under duress. Then I remembered I should be relieved, not pissed about handing over my baked goods.

"So?" Shaye asked. "How was it?"

"He was a little uncomfortable at first—like I said, he's a bit stiff." Tamara sat up straighter. "But when he finally put his lips to mine, let's just say ladies, he got a lot less boring."

"So you enjoyed it?" I asked.

She fanned herself. "You have *seen* the prince, haven't you?"

"Of course. But you said he was dull."

"Until we kissed," Tamara corrected me. "*Chest* is much more interesting than *chess*."

I didn't say anything. I couldn't. She'd literally rendered me speechless.

"Anyway, try not to be too jealous when you see the episode. He got a bit handsy." She popped a piece of turkey into her mouth. "Yum. How juicy. Just like His Highness."

This time, Shaye actually started to choke, so Blake whacked her on the back.

And I just sat there, not knowing whether to laugh or cry.

꧁꧂

"MISS. MISS," EVANGELINE WHISPERED URGENTLY. "Wake up."

I groggily opened my eyes. It was still dark in my room.

"What's the matter? Is it the rebels? Is it my sister?"

"Everything's okay." Evangeline bustled about a bit breathlessly, laying out clothes and packing a bag. "But His Highness sent word that your sister has taken a turn for the worse. I'm so sorry, miss. But the doctor said you should come home and see her."

My eyes welled with tears. "Is she dying?"

Evangeline rushed over and hugged me. "They didn't say that. Take heart. But the prince wanted you to be able to see her."

"O-Okay." I dressed quickly, my mind going a million miles a minute, accomplishing nothing but worry.

Once we'd hastily assembled an overnight bag, I hugged Evangeline one more time then hustled down the stairs. Two guards waited for me, bowing when I reached the foyer. "Miss. We're to take you to Settlement Four. We'll be there first thing in the morning."

"T-Thank you." My whole body thrummed with adrenaline.

"Wait." Boots clacked against the stones behind us, and Dallas emerged from the darkness. "I'm coming with you. Take Miss West to the car, I'll join you in a moment."

My brain scrambled. A car? None of the settlements had had access to fuel or vehicles since the war. I hadn't even seen a car in ages.

We headed outside, and I stopped dead in my tracks. "That's not a car," I whispered, "that's a *tank*."

One of the guards took my bag and smiled gently. "It's what they used to call a Sport Utility Vehicle. It's very good on the back roads."

I peered inside the cavernous space when he opened the door. The seats were sturdy dark leather. The guards got into the two front seats, and I sat in the back, heart pounding in the darkness.

Dallas opened the door a moment later, climbing in next to me. I was relieved to see him but worried. 4 was hours away.

"Can you really come with me?"

He laced his fingers through mine. "You're my priority."

My heart swelled, and my eyes stung.

He ran his thumb along the back of my hand. "I want to be there to help, if you need me. And we'll come back directly. My father and advisors will simply have to understand."

"What about Tariq?" The royal emissary would be bent out of shape that his star had left the premises.

"I don't give a flying fig about Tariq."

"Thank you for coming." It meant more to me than I could put into words. "What did the doctor say?"

Even in the car's dim lighting, I could see his face tighten. "Your sister's not responding to the fluids they're giving her. The fever hasn't broken."

I scrunched my eyes shut, hoping to stop the flow of tears. Instead, they spilled over, streaking my cheeks. "O-Okay. Maybe she'll get better, though. Maybe the medicine will start to work."

"Oh, Gwyneth. I hope so."

"I'm just so happy I get to go see her, the poor thing. She's only seven."

I lost it. My shoulders shook with sobs, and Dallas put his arm around me, pulling me close. "It's okay. It's going to be okay."

I wanted to believe him. I wanted to believe him so badly.

CHAPTER 10
FEVER PITCH

I COULDN'T SLEEP. DALLAS AND I SAT NEXT TO EACH other, hands entwined, staring out our respective windows, lost in our own thoughts. At one point, the guards pulled over to refuel the vehicle. "Do you want to stretch your legs?" Dallas asked.

I shook my head. I didn't want to talk, and I didn't want to move. All I wanted was to see Winifred.

If she died... If I lost her...

I banished the thoughts from my head. I'd be no use to my family if I arrived a sobbing, blathering mess. I'd finally cleaned myself up and pulled myself together. I refused to start crying again. I might not stop.

Dallas kept his arm around me, and I rested against his chest. I took so much comfort in his presence—his warmth, his scent, his big arm around my shoulder. I nestled against him, feeling safe and protected, even as my nerves thrummed.

Finally, as the sun broke over the horizon, we crossed into Settlement 4. Hours north from the palace, winter's mark was still heavy on the landscape. The grass sparkled, covered in frost, and the trees were bare. I shivered, looking at my home district. How was my family surviving without me? Did they have enough wood? Had the house gotten too cold, and was that why Winifred had gotten sick? I sat up straighter, throat tightening and body shaking with adrenaline as we headed to the downtown district. Dallas stared out the window with interest, his dark gaze taking in every detail.

"Have you been here before? To Settlement Four?"

"No." His face twisted. "My father's made it a priority to keep me out of the settlements. He doesn't think it's safe. But now that I see what's out here, I think maybe there was another reason." His brow furrowed as he saw some homeless people, huddled together under a bridge.

"Are you safe here?"

Dallas chuckled without humor. "I'm quite safe. I'll explain that to you at some point, but for now, do not concern yourself with me."

I nodded, all jittery. I gave the driver directions, and we pulled into my neighborhood. Formerly quite posh, the townhouses had fallen into disrepair since the war. I was quite shocked to see royal sentinels lining the streets, all standing at attention. A full guard was assembled outside my house.

"Your physician travels with security?" I asked Dallas.

His full, luscious lips set in a grim line. "They're for me."

"Ah." We parked in front of my house. Compared to the castle, the place was positively dingy. Still, I held my head high as the guard opened the door and held out his hand for me. It didn't matter what my home looked like. What mattered were the people who lived there.

So close to them, my heart pounded.

Dallas came to the sidewalk and clasped my hands. "Are you all right with me coming in? I can wait outside."

"Oh, no, please come with me. You're the reason I'm here." I stared at the front door, dreading what might be inside. "And I would like to have you near."

He looked as if he melted a little, but then he released my hands and respectfully stood behind, letting me go first.

My mouth went completely dry as I climbed the steps and knocked on the door. "Mother? It's me." I licked my lips. "Gwyneth."

A guard opened the door and bowed. "Miss West. Your Highness. We've been expecting you."

I hustled past him.

"Gwyneth? In here," my mother called from the living room.

I ran to them.

I noticed, without really looking, that there were guards stationed around the room. My brother played on the rug, and my mother sat near my sister. The doctor spoke in low tones to a nurse. A fire roared in the fireplace.

Winnie was on the couch, pale, so pale, with two hectic spots of color in her cheeks. She slept, chest rising and falling, but for some reason, her breathing looked strained. An IV dripped into her forearm.

Remy sat on the floor with his blocks, his eyes wide. "Gwyny!" He reached up for me, and I swept him into my arms, hugging him and kissing his face until he started to squirm.

"I missed you, you little bugger." I gently set him down and turned to my mother, who knelt on the floor beside Winnie. Dark circles bloomed like bruises underneath her eyes. Her hair was pulled back sharply, and her face looked thin.

"Mother."

She hugged me fiercely. "It's so good of you to come." She was never one for tears, and her voice was even and steady.

I turned to my sister and brushed the hair back from her forehead. Her skin was hot to the touch. "Tell me everything."

My mother sighed. "It happened at the end of last week. It came on suddenly. She was fine, then she woke up in the middle of the night with a high fever. You know children always start a fever at night. The next morning, she seemed better, but by the end of the day, she was lethargic—didn't want to eat, didn't want to drink, didn't want to play—totally unlike your sister. So I called Dr. Northman, and he diagnosed flu. But there's nothing he could do about it, and he didn't have any medicine for her. But then Dr. Cameron showed up." She motioned to the female doctor across the room. "She started IVs. But Winnie hasn't woken up, and her fever hasn't broken. It's still over a hundred and seven."

I winced. "The poor thing."

My mother straightened her spine, smoothed her dress, and looked around the room, blinking. Her gaze settled on the prince, and she quickly rose. "Oh, I've quite forgotten myself! Your Highness." She curtsied, and I marveled at her ability to bring it. She likely hadn't slept for days, and she was still light on her feet. "Thank you so much for sending help and for bringing Gwyneth here. It means so much to all of us."

Dallas stepped into the room, looking extremely tall, royal, and out of place. He bowed and took my mother's hand. "It's an honor to meet you, my lady. I'm so sorry your daughter's ill."

"Thank you, Your Highness."

Remy peered around my mother. He looked up at the prince, a solemn expression on his face.

Dallas smiled at him. "You must be Remy."

"I saw you on the TV," Remy said without preamble.

Dallas laughed. "Did you see your sister, too?"

Remy nodded. "She looked weird."

"Remy." My mother frowned at him.

Remy ignored her, as usual. He kept staring at Dallas. "You're tall."

"I am quite tall," Dallas said agreeably.

"C'mere." I held out my arms to Remy, and he ran to me. I lifted him up. "Have you been helping Mother?"

He nodded. Still, I noticed the firewood supply was low. I'd have to speak to them about that, but this wasn't the time.

"Do you feel okay?" I asked my brother.

He nodded. "The doctor gave me the flu test. I don't have it."

I hugged him fiercely. "Good. Good boy. I'm going to visit with Winnie for a minute, but then I'll come and play with you, okay? I've missed you so much." I kissed him again, and even though he wiped it off, he grinned.

"Little monster."

I set him down, and he immediately returned to his blocks, talking to himself in earnest. Remy's pretend games lasted for hours. With the cold Settlement 4 winters, it was a blessing he could entertain himself.

I turned my attention to my sister, grasping her hand in mine.

"Hello, Winnie. It's me, Gwyn." I squeezed her hand. "You'll never guess who's here. The *prince*. He brought me all the way from the castle just to see you."

My shoulder was squeezed, and I looked up to see Dallas. He briefly rubbed my back as he made his way to the doctor.

"Dr. Cameron, Your Highness, please join me in the kitchen for tea." My mother bustled off, and I wondered if she had any fine cups left to serve them with. This was exactly the sort of thing that would cause her grief, but I couldn't care less.

"Gwyneth." Dallas was the last one to leave the room. "I'm here if you need me."

I nodded, touched by his continued kindness. "Thank you."

I clutched Winnie's hand as they left the room. "You'd love the prince," I told her. "He's *very* chivalrous and tall and handsome, of course, just like you said. He took me riding the other day. My horse's name was Maeve. She was pure white, so sweet and strong. Oh, the horses, Winnie, you would love them..."

Comforted by the sound of my little brother playing on the rug next to me, and the feel of my sister's hand in mine, I relaxed at being unexpectedly home. I'd missed my family more than I could say. I intermittently reached over and ruffled Remy's hair while I prattled on and on, hoping that I could somehow reach my sister, wherever she was.

Don't you leave me, Winnie. It's not your time. Not yet.

CHAPTER 11
WINGS WOULDN'T HELP YOU

"Charge! They're headed our way!"

I woke up, stiff and confused, to find Dallas on the carpet with Remy, playing...toy soldiers?

"I've got them now!" Remy manipulated his action figure around the block castle they'd constructed.

"Good boy. You've got them cornered." Dallas grinned at my brother then raised his eyes to meet mine. "Hello, Gwyneth."

I smiled at him. "Hello, Your—Dallas."

Remy frowned at us but then looked past me. "Winnie?"

I turned sharply and found my sister blinking her eyes.

"Dr. Cameron," I yelled, "Dr. Cameron!"

"Your sister is going to be just fine." Dr. Cameron patted my arm, reassuring me one last time.

I didn't want to leave her, to leave them. But we'd stayed all day, and even though he hadn't said a word, I knew the prince had to get back. His father was likely boiling mad he'd been gone so long, not to mention Tariq. Not to mention the other girls.

"Thank you, Doctor. I appreciate everything you've done."

Dr. Cameron tucked one of her tiny braids behind her ear and smiled. "It's my pleasure. I'm meeting with Dr. Northman before we leave, and I'll make sure to leave specific follow-up instructions and plenty of medicine. But I don't think Winnie will need it. She's strong, and children her age bounce back surprisingly fast, unlike old ladies like me." She laughed.

"About the medicine." Dallas nodded at her. "When we get back to the palace, I'd like to speak with you about setting up clinics in all the settlements."

Dr. Cameron's eyes shone. "Your Highness, that would be amazing."

He nodded. "I'd like you to spearhead it. We'll talk more when we get back."

Dallas knelt down by my sister, who'd been watching him with wide eyes ever since she'd woken up. "Winfred, I'm so glad you're feeling better."

"Your Highness." She didn't even blink, as if she were afraid she'd miss something.

"Would it be acceptable for me to write to you? I'd like to keep in touch, so I know how you're doing."

Winnie's eyeballs almost popped out of her head. "Yes, Your Highness."

I giggled beneath my hand. She couldn't seem to get enough of saying "Your Highness."

He rose and bowed formally to her, then turned to my brother, holding out his hand for a high five. Remy slapped his hand hard.

"Remy!" I scolded.

Remy grinned at me. "I taught him how to do it. He likes it when I bring the heat."

They next performed some sort of fist bump, ending with each of them shaking their fingers like tambourines.

Dallas chuckled. "See you around, Remy."

Remy beamed at the prince. "Not unless I see you first."

"Remy. Don't be fresh." I held out my arms for him, and he pulled a face, but he came and gave me a hug. "Behave yourself. I love you."

"Love you, too." His words came out smushed because I was squeezing him so tight.

I let go of him and squatted down to his level. "One more thing."

"I know," Remy said. "The firewood."

"That's right. You can't let it get that low again. I don't want Winnie getting pneumonia. You're the man of the house now."

He nodded solemnly.

"I love you." I smooched him and hugged him again. "Now go play, and be a good boy."

I turned to my sister, brushing the hair from her face again. "I'm so glad you're better."

"You already said that," she said, sounding vaguely annoyed and much more like her old self. Her gaze flicked quickly to the prince. "He's awfully nice," she whispered.

I winked at her. "He *is* rather nice."

Her eyebrows quirked up, a thousand unanswered questions clearly running through her mind. But like my mother, she had the knack for the social decorum my brothers and I had always lacked. "Thank you for coming."

I squeezed her hand. "Thank you for getting better."

I kissed the top of her head, reluctant to leave her. "I'll write soon, okay?"

She nodded, smiling, and I felt infinitely relieved. *She made it. She was going to be okay.*

I looked up to find Dallas staring at me, a fact Winnie also eagerly took note of.

"I'm sorry we have to go," he said.

I held out my hand for him. "Don't be sorry. I'm just so glad we got to be here."

He waved to the kids as I dragged him into the kitchen to say goodbye to my mother. Her eagle eyes took in our entwined hands, and I dropped his immediately, embarrassed.

Dallas bowed to her. "Mrs. West, it was a pleasure. Thank you so much for having me in your home and for letting me meet your beautiful family."

My mother put a hand over her heart. "Oh, Your Highness, it was our pleasure. Thank you for saving my little girl."

Dallas bowed then regarded her when he stood. "I'd like your permission for something, my lady."

Her gaze flicked excitedly to me, and my stomach lurched.

"I'd like to leave the nurse here with you until Winifred is one-hundred percent."

My mother's face softened, even though that wasn't what she'd been hoping for. "That's very kind. Thank you."

"I'd also like to leave some guards in your service. They will stay at local headquarters, of course, but I'd like you to have security here around the clock. My men can also help with the household chores and the firewood, and they can oversee the extra provisions we'll be sending you from the palace."

My mother, rarely caught off guard, looked confused. "Extra provisions?"

Dallas nodded stiffly. "I'm sorry that the rations we've provided to date haven't been sufficient. I promise that the government will be more generous going forward. I'll see to it."

"Thank you." She curtsied, quickly recovering herself. "For everything."

I hugged her.

"I'll give you two a moment. I'll be in the car, Gwyneth." Dallas left us alone.

I pulled back, smiling at my mother. "You look tired. You should get some rest. She's going to be okay."

My mother blew out a deep breath. "Thank God."

I hugged her again, which was unusual for us, but no one loved Winnie like we did.

"I'll write soon, I promise. There are only four weeks left. And I'll be getting a stipend—"

"Gwyneth." My mother cut me off, gripping my hands in hers. "You must listen to me. The prince is in love with you."

My cheeks heated. "He likes me, I think—"

"He's not looking at you with like. It's more than that, as plain as day. And he brought you here in the middle of the night to see your sister. He genuinely cares for you."

She looked me straight in the eye. "Do you know what this could mean for our family?"

"Of course I do." I shook my hands free of her, of her pressure and her meddling and her expectations. "Why do you think I agreed to enter the competition in the first place?"

My mother frowned at me. "Think of what he just did for your sister, for all of us. He accomplished in one morning what we haven't had in five years: safety, security, the ease and hope that wealth brings to your life. We haven't had anything close since your father and Balkyn left, and I, for one, am tired of living like a scared pauper."

I took a deep breath, trying to calm myself so this didn't turn into a fight. "I don't understand your point."

"You're still young, Gwyneth. Young and headstrong. Your temper rules you."

"That's not true." My cheeks heated, and I felt it—my temper.

"A girl your age can't understand that there are things more important in life than your own feelings."

I gritted my teeth. "My family's the most important thing to me."

"Then I'm asking you, no matter what happens, think of us. The competition's going to be intense, but think of your family. And do not let the prince get away."

I groaned. "He's not a fish to be reeled in, Mother."

She arched an eyebrow. "But reel you must. And do not let go."

CHAPTER 12
TAKE A CHANCE ON ME

I WAS STILL SHAKING MY HEAD WHEN I CLIMBED INTO THE back of the car. No one could push my buttons like my mother. *No one.*

"What's the matter?" Dallas asked.

I sighed. "It's just my mother. I love her, but she drives me crazy."

He laughed. "I know the feeling."

I smiled politely. My mother was overbearing, but *his* mother was positively petrifying. I quickly changed the subject. "Why are all these people out here?"

I was surprised to see my neighbors out on their steps, curiously watching our car. More civilians lined the side-walks. There was no cheering, like in the propaganda videos; it was more the curious stares of strangers.

"Word's gotten out that we're here." Dallas watched the civilians from behind the dark-tinted windows.

"If they know it's us...shouldn't we wave or something?"

"Yes. We should." He sat forward immediately. "I never get out here, so I didn't even think about it." He instructed the driver to slow the vehicle, and we both rolled down our windows, waving to the people lining the streets. Now, they began to clap and smile.

"Gwyneth!" I saw my friend Lyra standing near the corner, waving and grinning. "Go, you!"

"I'll write you soon!" I leaned out of the window and blew her a kiss.

Dallas chuckled as a little girl, probably all of three, sitting on her father's shoulders waved at him madly. He waved back, and she shrieked in delight.

"Adorable," he said, but then he did a double take as he looked out the window. "The camera crew's following us."

I looked and saw another large vehicle following us, making its way slowly down the street. A cameraman stuck his head out the back window, filming the crowds.

We drove further out of town, and the audience thinned. I gave the vehicle behind us another look. "Did you tell them where we were going?"

He scrubbed a hand across his face. "I told several of my advisors and left a note for my father. I guess they must have alerted the crew."

"Hmm." I twisted the hem of my dress. "I guess we veered a little off the script." I had a feeling I'd be hearing about it from Tariq.

"You don't need to look worried. I'll deal with it. Besides, I expect that showing us under the circumstances —helping your sick sister—will be considered a PR coup by the team." He frowned.

"And that's bad because..."

He shrugged. "It's not bad. But that's not what this was about, and I get tired of the non-stop posturing."

"I bet."

He hit a button, and a screen rose up, separating us from the guards. "Privacy screen." Dallas smiled, and my heart skipped a beat.

He grabbed my hand. "I liked your family very much. Thank you for letting me meet them."

"Thank you for having Dr. Cameron save my sister's life and for bringing me to see her. That meant everything to me."

"See? I keep telling you—I'm not so bad." His eyes twinkled.

"My siblings are both obsessed with you, and my mother is obviously beside herself that you came to the house, which is my way of saying no, you're not so bad at all."

Dallas's face darkened. "Your mother seemed a bit embarrassed, actually, when she made us tea. She kept apologizing for her 'lacking' service. I felt terrible."

"I'm sure she was just being polite." Actually, she was probably mortified by our meager offerings.

"No, it's one of the reasons I mentioned the extra provisions. I saw inside your cupboards—they were bare."

He looked out the window, cursing under his breath. Then he was quiet for so long I didn't think he'd say more until he continued. "I'm so sorry, Gwyneth. Your family was not in good shape. They lacked food and heat. Your poor sister probably got sick because your house was freezing."

"It's my fault." I sighed. "I used to take care of the firewood, of everything. I babied them too much, and now they're having a hard time getting on because I'm not there."

He turned to me, face stormy. "They are children. You treated them as you should, by protecting them. But I, as their prince? I'm the one who's failed them. I've believed the lies my advisors have told me for far too long. The settlements are in much worse shape than I knew."

"But why would they keep it from you?"

It was beginning to dawn on me that we had several hours together in the car, and I could finally ask him all the questions that had been burning me up for the past few weeks.

Dallas frowned. "Before we conquered the settlements, my father promised me that we were doing it to bring a better life to the people who lived here. He assured me at every step that we would be lifting the people up and saving them from the rebels threatening their society from within."

"When you say rebels, do you mean the same rebels my father and brother left to fight for?"

Dallas winced. "It's complicated, Gwyneth. And there's much I can't tell you."

I filed this away to pester him about later and returned to his comments about the state of the settlements. "Why would your father want to hide the truth from you?"

"He does not want me to see how the people are really living. You told me before that the people suffered, but now I've seen it for myself."

I rubbed his hand. "You can't blame yourself. Now that you know, you will make changes. That's all anyone can ask."

He shook his head. "I've let myself be deceived for too long. I do not see things the way my father does..." He bit off the sentence, looking pained.

"Nor must you," I encouraged. "You will be king someday, and you will govern as you see fit."

Dallas's eyes blazed. "Sometimes, that day seems too far away."

"I think the idea about the clinics was great. You can still make important improvements as the prince. You can help the people in the settlements."

"It's long overdue, I'm afraid." Dallas would not be comforted.

"Then there's no time like the present. Think of all the people you can help going forward."

He gave me a funny look. "My dearest Gwyneth, I do believe you're trying to make me feel better."

"Of course I am. You just saved my sister's life. As far as I'm concerned, you're my knight in shining armor. I want you to see yourself the way I see you right now."

"You've quite taken me off guard. I'm not used to this side of you." The corners of his lips tugged up. "I don't know what to say."

"Thank you?" I giggled.

He reached for my hands, gaze burning into mine. "Thank you."

"Since I have your favor, and we have an awfully long car ride, can we do something?"

He brushed the hair back from my face, looking quite, quite interested. He leaned closer, eyes glittering. "Anything."

His cool breath wafted over my face, practically making me pant. I willed my hormones to calm themselves, but I still shivered—from his closeness, from his scent, from his big hands surrounding mine.

"I want to ask you questions. About a million of them."

He dropped back against the seat, laughing. "I should've known."

"Since coming to the palace," I earnestly continued, "I've learned a lot of new things. For instance, that vampires are real. And then there's the bit about gnomes. Any way, I have a lot of questions. So may I ask them? And will you answer?"

He chuckled. "To the best of my ability."

I mentally rubbed my hands together. *So many subjects!*

"Excellent. Now, let me see…"

CHAPTER 13
CONFIDENCES

"SO... I HEARD YOU AND TAMARA PLAYED CHESS?"

"Here we go." Dallas groaned. "I'd rather start with the buggerish gnomes."

"We'll get to them." I laughed. "But first, Tamara told us about the wager."

"I didn't plan to kiss her, if that's what you're asking."

"It's not. She told us the whole story—her version, of course."

"Of course." He sighed. "I would not have chosen her for a second date, but some of these matters are out of my control."

"What do you mean?"

His gaze flicked to me. "You asked me for something, and now I must ask you for something in return."

"Yes?"

"Everything we talk about on this ride remains confidential. It must stay between us, Gwyneth. I mean it."

I nodded. "You have my word. Now, please, explain what you meant."

"Tariq and his group—the producers from the network —are largely running the Pageant. They mostly tell me what to do, and I do it, as long as I don't have some sort of moral objection."

I bristled. "Does that mean they picked me as your first date? And as your first *second* date?"

"I picked you." Dallas gently but firmly laced his fingers through mine. "Our interactions have been legitimate. The rest of the proceedings are mostly staged. They have me going through the motions with a smile on my face."

"But you still kissed Shaye," I blurted out.

He sighed. "Yes, I still kissed Shaye."

"I should let that go, I suppose." I wanted to, but part of my brain—the prefrontal cortex? I'd learned about it at the academy—was still too young and unformed to handle such a sophisticated maneuver. So I throbbed with hot jealousy any time I thought of the prince with my pretty friend.

"Yes, you should let it go." He leaned forward. "Because my hand is around yours right now. Not only that, I just met your family not too long ago because *we drove through the night to see them*. And I chose *you* for my first second date, not Shaye. Because for some reason, I cannot seem to stay away from you, no matter how often you yell at me and stomp off—which, I might remind you, you did right before that very date."

I cleared my throat, not knowing what the bloody hell to say. He had me there. "I see."

He leaned back a bit, hand still clamped around mine. "Do not doubt me, Gwyneth."

Chills needled down my spine. "I do not, Dallas."

He seemed to calm down. He tugged on my hand. "Proceed with your questions. I'm afraid I've lost track."

"Back to Tamara."

He groaned again. "Tariq wanted her for the next second date. She has a loyal following in the audience. He said she shows well on television and that her family's influential. So not only is she good for ratings, she's good for politics."

"I can see that." Tamara was beautiful, and she was never close to dull. "Her wager was if she won the chess match, you would kiss her."

"Yes. Were you asking me a question?"

"How was it? The kiss?"

"It was...kiss-ish." He pulled a face, and I swatted him.

"I mean it. She said it was dreamy. I want to know how you would describe it."

He shrugged. "It was fine."

"Fine?"

He shrugged again.

"She said you got a bit handsy."

Dallas laughed so suddenly and hard I thought he might choke.

"Oh, I bet she did," he said when he'd recovered. "I can't believe you fall for her tricks. She's playing you—and quite well, I must add."

"So you didn't get, er...handsy?"

Dallas looked thoughtful. "If I remember correctly, she put her arms here." He took my hands and placed them around his broad shoulders, and I fastened them at the base of his neck.

"And I put mine here." He put a large palm on each of

my hips then flexed his fingers. He pulled me closer. "Just like this."

He gazed down into my eyes, his face inches from mine.

"Oh." Suddenly the car had gotten very, very hot. "I see."

He shrugged, suddenly releasing me, a roguish grin on his face. "At least, that's how I remember it."

"Oh...you...you are..."

He arched an eyebrow. "Is that a question?"

I groaned while he chuckled. "No."

I forced myself to recover—resisting the urge to fan myself or pummel him. "Moving on. I want to ask you about vampires and being a vampire."

He smiled at me lazily, clearly enjoying the effect he had on me. "I'm listening."

I primly cleared my throat. "You said before that you can become a vampire one of two ways: born a vampire or turned. Is that correct?"

"Yes. I was born this way. Others, like Eve, are turned."

"So your parents had you biologically? The way humans have babies?"

"Yes, although the gestation period is longer for vampires. My mother carried me in her womb for twelve months instead of nine. You can't rush greatness, of course." He chuckled.

"Ha ha. But you were a baby, and you grew, just like a human?"

"Yes, but biological vampires only mimic humans to a point. Each year, I grew larger and stronger, passing through stages of development the same way a human child does. But when I turned twenty, that changed. I am still physically twenty, but I've aged in years."

My brow furrowed. "I don't understand."

"I'm older than I look. But I'll stay physically twenty for several decades or a bit longer, and then my body will age a bit more, and so on and so on. Aging is a much more protracted process for a vampire than a human. It takes you decades. It takes us centuries."

"How old are you, exactly?" I peered at him.

"Older than you. But not by so very much."

"Hmm." So he would age, but not nearly as quickly as I would. The length of my human life would be a blip on his radar. "How old is your father?"

"Very old. So old that I won't tell you because you would only have a billion more questions to ask, and the car ride isn't long enough to answer them."

"And your mother?"

He sat back a bit. "My mother's different. She was turned. Those who are turned remain physically the same as the time of their transformation. So she looks young, but she's actually quite a bit older than my father."

"So... Eve will always look the same?"

"Yes. As will my mother, as will my friend Lucas, as will many of the Black Guard you've seen at the palace."

"But you will age and change, as will your father."

"That's right."

I nodded, trying to process all the information. "So you will grow old?"

"Yes. Eventually."

"But will you die? Sorry to ask such a morbid question. But Eve keeps talking about her immortality—does that mean you *cannot* die?"

Dallas blew out a deep breath. "Remember, Gwyneth, what I said about keeping this a confidence?"

I nodded.

"I'm only going to tell you this because I trust you, and I believe you deserve to know the truth. I'm trusting you with my life and my family's. I know that your brother and father are with the resistance, and I do not blame them—or you—because they couldn't have known the whole story. But this type of information cannot be shared, or the rebels will use it against us."

I started to butt in with more questions, but he held up his hand. "I won't tell you everything on this trip. Not about the rebels, not about the settlements, not all of it. I can't. It would be too dangerous for you. Not only that, but there isn't time."

I nodded, biting my tongue, willing him to continue.

"Back to your question: yes, vampires can die. We can be killed. The old stories are true—a stake to the heart can do it. Some of us can die from prolonged exposure to sunlight. I'm not one of them. Others can be weakened to the point of near death by sunlight, which makes us susceptible to pain and being captured. Oh, and silver is bad for all vampires. But there must be a lot of it to have any sort of effect."

I frowned. "But none of the rebels even tried to stake you or capture you with silver. All they did was shoot."

He shook his head. "Those were some particularly dumb rebels."

When I grimaced, he put his hand over mine. "Humans are not fast enough to stake us. Other vampires can do it, but humans can only do it if we've been weakened by the sun or a large amount of silver or if they catch us unawares, which is highly unlikely."

"So they were shooting because they thought they could at least slow you down?"

He raked a hand through his hair. "My understanding is that not all the rebels believe what they've heard about us. They haven't yet learned our true weaknesses. That group thought they could take us with weapons. They were misinformed. It cost them their lives."

"I see." But really, I didn't. There were so many moving pieces. "So if you aren't staked in the heart, you will live forever?"

"Yes." His voice was gentle. "I know it's a lot to understand."

"Yes, but I want to know more." I paused for a moment, cheeks reddening. "Can vampires... Can they have a child with a human?"

Dallas's gaze locked with mine. "Yes."

The car was getting hot again.

"And would the child be a human or a vampire?"

"It would be an intercross."

Did I imagine it, or was he blushing?

"Does an intercross drink blood, or eat food?"

"I think it varies. They're quite rare."

"So you've never seen one?"

"I have, but only a few. Human and vampire unions are few and far between."

"Were there no humans up north, where you come from?"

He shook his head slightly. "No."

I filed that away to think about later. "Tell me more about the intercross."

"Like the rest of us vampires, there's quite a variety of

characteristics for each of them. Intercrosses are like snowflakes—no two are alike."

I pondered this for a moment, churning the information over in my mind. There was so much I'd never even thought of, never considered.

"So you will... You will marry a human girl. One chosen from the Pageant." I tried to keep my voice steady.

"Yes."

"And will you turn her—the winner—so that she may have the protections that you have as a vampire?"

"No." His answer was swift, without hesitation.

"Why not?"

"Because I would never turn a human. I don't believe in it."

"Why not?" I asked again.

He sighed. "It's not a choice a human can make. It should be informed consent, and that's not possible."

"I don't understand."

"There's no way a human can truly understand the consequences of becoming a vampire, so they cannot truly give informed consent. That's one of the reasons I was so appalled by what my mother did to Eve. She took her by force, and that was wrong, so wrong. Eve would never have chosen to be a vampire. She despised us."

"But she's very happy now. She told me she loves being a vampire."

"Eve is special. But don't let her fool you—her reaction to her transformation was difficult, at first. It's very hard to let go of your human life."

"But she's managed, and she's thriving."

Dallas traced an outline on my palm. "Yes, she's made

the best of it. She has a knack for seeing the bright side of things. She's amazing, really. She believes her transformation was meant to be. She wants to help people and vampires."

"That's what she told me, as well." I watched his fingers as they trailed along the lines of my palm.

"It's not like that for everyone."

"But what if your wife wanted to be changed?" I persisted. "What if she went through all the pros and cons and still chose to become a vampire?"

He shook his head. "She wouldn't. Being a vampire isn't exactly a walk in the park, Gwyneth. Being human is so much easier."

"Why? I don't think being human is easy. We're weak. We get old, and we get sick. We're vulnerable to many more things than the odd stake or the sun."

He took my palm in between both of his. "But humans can die. Everything is so much simpler when you can die."

"Why do you say that?"

He turned to look out the window, at the falling darkness. "Because when you have eternity, you have until the end of time to regret. And who would choose that?"

CHAPTER 14
OVER MY HEAD

I HEARD THE DESPAIR IN HIS VOICE, PLAIN AS DAY.

"What is it that you regret?"

"Didn't you see all the rebels I killed when they attacked? Not to mention Benjamin Vale? I ended his life in seconds." His shoulders were stiff. "That's a tiny fraction of what wrong I've done. You don't want to know what I regret."

I reached for him, but he was still and cold beneath my touch. "I know you. It hasn't been for long. But it's for long enough to know that you're a good person."

He shook his head, still looking out the window. "I'm not a person, nor am I good."

"I respectfully disagree, Your Highness." I rubbed his back, much like I would a skittish horse. "You just saved my baby sister out of the kindness of your heart."

He chuckled darkly. "It was a bit more self-interested than that."

My cheeks flushed, but I kept trying to soothe him. "Self-interested or not, you are good. I know it."

He turned and captured my hand underneath his. "Don't be so sure."

"But I am." My heart, every inch of me, believed in his goodness.

His eyes flashed. "I don't know what I've done to deserve this."

"What?" I asked, unsure of his meaning.

"This twist of fate." He kissed my hand.

I fought to keep my composure. "Perhaps you're better than you give yourself credit for, so fate is being kind."

"Wouldn't it be lovely," he asked, tapping my chin with his finger and turning my face up to his, "if that were true?"

I opened my mouth to answer, but Dallas leaned closer. Our eyes locked. Electricity zipped between us.

The question had changed. And oh, so had the answer.

His gaze burned. "May I?"

I nodded, and Dallas tentatively put his lips to mine.

I kissed him back, slowly at first, relishing the feel of his big, strong body against mine. He sank his hands deep into my hair and pulled me closer, so I was almost on his lap. His scent washed over me as our tongues connected. My heart thudded in my chest as I deepened the kiss, daring to run my hands over his broad shoulders.

He pulled back, his dark gaze raking over me.

"Wait," I said breathlessly. "Where are you going?"

He chuckled, momentarily putting some space between us. "I need to be a gentleman. You said I was your knight in shining armor. I can't be that *and* a rogue in the back seat of an SUV."

"Sure you can," I blurted out.

He laughed again. "Your honor, my lady, is as important to me as your safety. I vow to protect both."

I wrinkled my nose. "Ugh. I really hope you reconsider that."

His unexpected bark of laughter had me giggling, and some of the tension between us dissipated.

"We'll be back to the palace in a few short hours. You should really try to get some rest." He sat back against the seat and settled me against him, putting his muscular arm around my shoulders.

"I don't want to sleep," I objected, even as I nestled against him. "I want to ask more questions. Or resume...the other stuff."

But my voice was already thick. I'd slept for only one hour of the past twenty-four.

"Sleep. That's a command." Dallas chuckled as he stroked my hair.

Surrounded by his warmth and a largely unfamiliar sense of well being, I fell instantly to sleep.

⁂

"GWYNETH."

I curled my hands up near my face, snuggling deeper.

"We'll be at the palace in a minute. You should wake up before the cameras get to us." Dallas still held me close.

I moaned and wrapped my arms around his broad chest. "You're quite comfortable, for someone so large."

"Large? Is that an insult?"

"Mmm, I like it. You make me feel safe."

Dallas shifted beneath me, and I forced my eyes open so that I could look at him.

He smiled at me, his full, sensuous lips parting. "I've been thinking about something."

I sat up, unable to stop staring at his handsome face and those lips. How, in such a few weeks, had he become so important to me? Everything had changed. The center of my gravity had shifted, and I needed to get my bearings.

"Gwyneth?"

"Yes?" I adjusted my hair and smoothed my dress, trying to come back to my senses.

But I knew the truth. Everything was different.

"I was telling you I've been thinking about something."

I nodded, as if I'd been listening. "Of course. Go on."

He frowned, watching me smooth my dress again. "It's about us."

I looked up, now paying perfect attention. "Yes?"

He sighed, looking uncomfortable. "I hope to have more time with you once we're back at the palace."

"But?"

His eyes darkened. "But it won't be for a while. This trip was unscripted. I'm going to have to catch up on work, and I expect they're going to have me busy with the production schedule they have lined up."

I nodded. "You mean, all the dates you have to go on."

Dallas sighed. "Yes."

"You'll have lots of first dates and second dates to attend to, and I've already had both."

"Yes." He looked down at our entwined hands. "But I wanted to ask you for something."

"Of course."

He raised his gaze to meet mine. "I would like to kiss you in front of the cameras. I hope you will not object."

Objecting was not foremost on my mind—kissing him was.

But snogging for the cameras was something altogether

different. My nerves thrummed at the thought. "Um, I... Erm..."

"Let me explain. I will not have time with you again soon, and I want the cameras to see—to see what we have. Because it's important to me."

"Oh, Dallas. That's so sweet."

His gaze burned into me. "It's not all sweet. I assure you."

He took my face in his hands and lowered his lips to mine again.

At that moment, the privacy window rolled down. "Your Highness, we'll be pulling up to the palace shortly. We just wanted to make sure you were both ready."

Dallas dropped his hands from me and cursed. "Bloody hell, I know where we are!"

The driver coughed and looked at the other guard. "I'm sorry, my lord. You had asked me to remind you."

Dallas composed himself quickly. "I remember. I was just...speaking to Miss West. We'll be ready." He put the divider back up. "My apologies." He raked a hand through his hair, making it stand up in wild spikes.

The car rolled to a stop, and I sighed. The castle's stone facade was as beautiful and cold as ever. Servants lined the steps, waiting to welcome the prince back. The camera crew scrambled out of the vehicle behind us and hastily set up their equipment on the lawn.

Tariq stood on the stairs, a sour look on his face as he peered at our vehicle.

My stomach flipped. "Tariq's not going to be happy, is he?"

Dallas reached back and squeezed my hand. "You don't

need to worry about him or anything else. I'll take care of it."

The king came out and stood next to Tariq, and they huddled together, speaking about something.

"That can't be good." Dallas frowned as he watched them.

"I'd offer to protect you from them, but I expect that'd be cold comfort." I squeezed his hand again. "So I'll offer this instead: no matter what happens, I'm here for you. You've shown me so much kindness, Dallas. I won't forget it."

He turned and brushed the hair back from my face then gently put his hands on each of my cheeks. His eyes searched mine, looking for an answer to his silent question.

Yes. Always. "Please."

Dallas swiftly, hungrily put his lips to mine, devouring me with a deep kiss.

I moaned and arched my back, trying to pull him as close as I could.

When he finally released me, we were both breathing hard. He shook his head. "That was..." He seemed at a loss for words.

"Intense."

"Yes, it was." He fastened his dark gaze on me. "And it was just for us. I'll be much more restrained for the cameras."

Too riled up to be embarrassed, I fanned myself. "Sounds like a plan."

He glanced outside. "I don't want to say goodbye to you right now. I'd move into the back of this car with you, if you'd have me."

I melted, reaching out to stroke his face to comfort us

both. "I wish we didn't have to go. But this will be a happy memory for me while we have to be apart."

He pulled me in for one last, brief kiss, filled with longing. Then he placed his forehead against mine. "I'll be thinking of you at every moment."

"And I'll be thinking of you."

He released me, and we both straightened ourselves. He blew out a deep breath and held out his hand for me. "It's time."

I swallowed hard and nodded. Then I made myself take his hand, reluctantly leaving our happy little bubble behind.

CHAPTER 15
DON'T LET IT FOOL YOU

MIRA KINNEY SPRANG AT US AS SOON AS WE CLIMBED OUT of the car. "Your Highness, how was your visit to Settlement Four?"

Dallas kept his hand firmly around mine. "It was excellent. I met Miss West's family. They were lovely and hospitable. I'm happy to report that Miss West's younger sister is feeling much better."

"What wonderful news." Mira smiled at me, flashing all her teeth. "Miss West, everyone at the palace was so sad to hear that your little sister was ill. What was the diagnosis?"

She shoved the microphone under my nose, and the cameramen turned their klieg lights on me. I tried not to cringe, wondering how worn and mussed-up I must look. *That's not what's important.* Well aware that Tariq and the king were in the audience, I held my head high. I glanced at them briefly. The king watched me with thinly veiled distaste.

I took a deep breath. "Winnie had the flu. But thanks to His Highness, the royal family, and their staff, my sister was able to get the medical attention she needed. She's expected to make a full recovery. My family is so honored and thankful that the royal family has helped us in this way."

Mira beamed at me. *Well done*, she mouthed. "Were you surprised that the prince offered to bring you to Settlement Four to see your family?"

I nodded. "I was, but I shouldn't have been. His Highness is the most thoughtful, kind man I know."

"Why, Miss West." Dallas bowed to me. "Thank you."

I curtsied. "Your Highness. Thank *you*. For everything."

"It was my pleasure." He clasped my hands then leaned down and kissed me on the lips. It was brief, quite chaste compared to what we were getting up to before, but I still heard one of the servants on the stairs gasp.

Dallas released me and turned back to the cameras. "And now that we're back, I've important business to attend to. Thank you all for the warm welcome."

He nodded to me one last time then released me. With a turn of his heel and the flourish of his cape, he went to join Tariq and his father.

Mira Kinney and the camera crew packed up. The staff curtsied and bowed as the royals swept up the stairs with Tariq nipping at their heels. They hustled back inside the palace, eager to carry on with their business.

I stood for a moment, watching them. My heart suddenly felt heavy. I begrudgingly climbed the stairs, missing my family, missing the prince, missing the warmth and cozy security of the car. I was back in the game. But having been home and then having the prince all to myself for those precious hours, I felt more alone than ever.

EVANGELINE INTERCEPTED ME ON MY WAY TO THE common room. "Miss. Miss!"

She waved me over then stood there, wringing her hands.

"Is everything all right?"

She quickly curtsied. "Yes, of course. But I thought you might like to change after such a long ride. I'll have the guards bring up your bag." She nodded to them then hustled me up the stairs. "I'm so happy to hear your sister's better. What a blessing."

"Yes, it is. It was lovely to see my family." We made small talk as we headed to my chambers.

I waited until we were safely inside my room to ask again. "Is everything really all right?"

"It is, but I thought I would have a word before you went and saw all the other girls."

"Uh oh." I braced myself. "Am I to guess that they aren't pleased with me at the moment?"

"I heard something to that effect." She bit her lip. "I don't like to gossip, but I've heard that Tamara's been saying all manner of things, getting the other girls all riled up."

I put my hands on my hips, feeling the dull throb of a headache coming on. "Thank you for letting me know. I'll be prepared to handle it now."

Evangeline nodded, but I sensed there was more on her mind.

"Is there something else?"

"I also heard that—and I don't know if it's true—but I heard that one of the human prisoners killed a guard and escaped."

Several of the rebels had been captured during the last

attack. They'd been kept in the cells below the castle ever since.

I put a hand over my heart. "Oh, no. That's terrible."

"Normally, the prince would say something to the staff about it, but it's different when he's gone. The king and queen are more private, I guess."

"I feel terrible." Dallas was the person who kept the castle running smoothly. He had an excellent relationship with the staff. I'd taken him away from home when he'd been needed.

She patted my arm. "You shouldn't, miss, it's nothing to do with you. But I heard we might have stricter rules again, like the curfew, and more guards around the palace. I just thought you should know."

"Thank you, Evangeline."

She smiled. "Now let's get you in a fresh dress, so you'll be ready for Tamara and the rest of them."

I smiled back, but it felt forced. Tamara was a pain in the butt.

But an escaped rebel was much, much worse.

CHAPTER 16

BEASTLY

"A WORD, MISS WEST." TARIQ CAUGHT UP TO ME IN the hall.

I nodded, bracing myself for a chewing out. I followed him into a small study, and he closed the door behind us. He immediately started pacing, his hands clasped behind his back.

"I've just come from a meeting with King Black and the prince."

I waited for him to continue, but he let that self-important piece of news hang in the air for a moment.

Finally, I caved. "Yes, Your Royal Emissary?"

"The King's very unhappy that the prince left the premises and traveled to Settlement Four without his express permission."

I nodded. "I understand. I hope the prince isn't in too much trouble."

"He's not, thanks largely to me." He stopped pacing and watched me. "I sent the camera crews after you, of course.

They were in touch while in Four, raving about the footage they were getting. The settlers were wild to have the prince among them, and they worship him for saving your sister. His approval ratings are off the chart in your section of Four."

"So that's good."

Tariq frowned at me.

"Or not?"

He resumed pacing. "We're putting together the episode tonight. We want the people in every settlement to know how kind the prince is, how much he cares for his people."

"Again, that's good."

"What is *not* good is the disproportionate amount of time the prince has spent with you. It's unfair to the other girls. Some of them threatened to leave after this last escapade, saying that they weren't receiving equal treatment."

"It wasn't an escapade. My sister was very ill." I struggled to keep my voice even. "But I know that D—His Royal Highness—needs to spend time with each contestant. He told me as much. I know he won't have time for me in the next few weeks. I understand that, and I'm prepared for it."

Tariq's eyes glittered. "That's not the only problem."

"Yes?"

"The king has voiced his disapproval of you." He watched me as he delivered the blow. "He's aware of your family's connection to the rebels and also of your involvement with the prisoner Benjamin Vale."

"I would think he'd hold *you* responsible for some of this."

Tariq narrowed his eyes. "Tread carefully, Gwyn."

I stood my ground. "I was brought to the palace by invitation, if you'll remember—your invitation. It's on you that you didn't properly background check the contestants. Look at what happened with Eve!"

In her human life, Eve had been an outspoken opponent of the vampires. That's what had gotten her bit by the queen—her views, and her inability to keep her mouth shut even when it was dangerous.

Tariq pursed his lips. "I thought you might say that. But right now, we're talking about you. And you should know, not only did the king express his displeasure with the prince's unexcused absence, he also disapproves of the prince's seeming preference for you over the other girls."

Heat flooded my cheeks. "And what did the prince say to that?"

"He said that he does not favor you. He said he chose to take the trip to Settlement Four to help your sister but also because it was good public relations."

Because Tariq was clearly watching me for signs of distress, I kept my features indifferent. I shrugged, hoping that Dallas had only said this to divert attention from me. "My sister was saved. That's the important thing."

Tariq continued as if I hadn't spoken. "When the king asked him why he'd chosen you for his first second date, the prince told him that *I* had arranged it."

I kept my face blank, but I couldn't stop the blushing. "So?"

"*So* that's a lie, which means he's protecting you, which means that we all need to proceed with caution."

"I don't understand what you mean."

"It means we're in a bit of a triangle." Tariq smiled at me, but it was not a nice smile. "It means that I'm charged with protecting you, too—protecting your little secret from the king."

"There's no secret. I'm not hiding anything."

He crossed his arms against his chest. "But the prince is."

"I don't see it that way." I couldn't wait to tell Dallas about this transgression. He would see Tariq's head roll.

Tariq leveled me with a stare. "What *I* see is that you clearly have the prince's favor. It would be a pity if the king prevented you from continuing in the contest."

"Speak plainly, Tariq."

He leaned forward and batted his long eyelashes at me. "Do not breathe a word of this conversation to the prince. If you do, I'll head straight for the king. And mark me; I have his ear. He'll listen when I tell him that Dallas only has eyes for you. And he won't be happy about it. In fact, he might be unhappy enough to have you sent home. And then the prince will propose to one of the other contestants, while you're stuck in miserable Four for the rest of your life."

I resisted the urge to smack him. "Four is hardly miserable."

He arched an eyebrow. "So you say."

I sighed, tired of him, tired of his rabid, ceaseless posturing. "Let me see if I've got this straight: I don't say a word to the prince, and you don't say a word to the king."

"That's right."

"But what's the point of all this?" I cried. "We're locked in a study, and you're fluttering your eyelashes and maneuvering. I don't understand what you're trying to accomplish."

"I wanted to be clear. I am happy to support you in the

contest and keep your secrets, but you must also support me."

"I told you before—if you helped me, I would help you." I'd asked a favor of Tariq and had him organize a special lunch for Dallas and me. I'd told him in return, I would voice my support for him with the prince. "But I'm going to be quite a bit less happy about it after the way you've spoken to me tonight."

"I'm doing it for a reason." Tariq's voice was tight. "You don't understand. There's a lot at stake in the competition."

I straightened my spine. "I understand perfectly. You think this competition is going to make or break your career with the royal family. And you will use any leverage you can find to shore up your position."

"Then I suppose you're not as dull-witted as I thought." He shrugged. "The point is, I have leverage over *you*. And I can make or break you."

I'd asked him to speak plainly, and now I regretted it.

"At some juncture, you might be in a unique position to help me. So if I ask you for a favor, I need your word that you'll do it."

I lifted my chin. "I won't do something that I think is wrong."

He smiled, and this time, it reached his eyes. "Then we will have to see what you're made of, my lady."

I WAS STILL SHAKING BY THE TIME I MADE IT TO THE common room, unable to get Tariq's words out of my head. *I'll head straight for the king.*

The king, who did not approve of me. The king, to whom Dallas had lied in order to protect me.

Mark me; I have his ear.

I cursed Tariq, his stupid eyelashes, and his scheming. He would attempt to use me for something. I prayed it was nothing too horrible.

Dinner was just finishing up. I spied my favorite kitchen maid, Andrea, and she promised to bring me a full plate of food. Tonight's offering was creamy macaroni and cheese, asparagus with lemon, and biscuits. *Perhaps there is a God.*

I felt eyes on me, and I turned to find Tamara staring as if she'd just smelled something rotten. *Perhaps not.* I sighed, making my way toward our table. Shaye gave me a tight smile while Tamara gnawed on a raw carrot, giving me the once over.

"How's your sister?" Shaye asked.

"She's much better, thank you."

"That's good." Shaye was friendly as usual, but an awkward silence settled over our table as I sat down.

My gaze flicked to Tamara, who was still chewing. "And how are you, Tamara? Sore from your daily squat count?"

"I'm not sore." She arched an eyebrow. "But are you?"

"I'm sorry?"

She looked me up and down. "Since you're not that pretty, and you're really quite dull, I've been wondering what the prince sees in you, why he's running in circles, chasing his tail to take you back to your shit-hole of a settlement. And now I think I have an idea."

"Tamara. For the love of all things holy, stop it." Shaye closed her eyes and shook her head, as if she knew exactly what was coming.

"I don't think so." Tamara whipped her ponytail back around and resumed glaring at me.

I glared right back. "What, exactly, are you insinuating?"

"I think you've been giving it to the prince."

"Giving what?" I didn't understand at first, but then it dawned on me. "Ah, I see."

Shaye's face turned crimson. She stared at her plate.

"Is that what you both think?"

Shaye shook her head miserably, but she didn't say a word.

"That's absolutely what I think, and most of the other girls do, too. I bet you've been letting him have his way, and *that's* why you've been getting special treatment."

Andrea set a plate in front of me, caught one whiff of the conversation, and scurried away.

"So." I dug into my mac and cheese. "You think I've been riding The Royal Stallion."

Tamara tossed down her carrot. "I can't think of another explanation that makes sense."

"The prince *has* been a bit handsy, lately." I took another bite, enjoying the fact that Tamara's eyeballs were almost popping out of her head. "But when things got too intense, he told me that my virtue was of the utmost importance to him."

I buttered my biscuit and had a bite, slowly chewing, savoring it. "It's a pity," I said when I'd finished. "Because he *is* a rather good kisser, and I quite enjoyed having his hands on me. So I hope he eventually changes his mind."

I grabbed another biscuit and stood. "Well, I'd say it's been a pleasure, but..."

Tamara rolled her eyes, not looking sorry in the least.

My gaze shifted to Shaye. "I expected more from you, at least."

Her pretty face puckered. "Gwyn."

But I was already out the door, heading for my chambers as fast as I could. They could say what they wanted about me.

But I wouldn't let them hurt me.

And I sure as hell wouldn't let them see me cry.

CHAPTER 17
BRING IT ON

THERE WAS A KNOCK ON MY DOOR FIRST THING THE next morning. Evangeline bustled in, a note in her hands. She handed it to me then curtsied. Her quick gaze ran over my face, probably taking in my puffy eyelids. I would never admit it, but I'd cried myself to sleep.

"I'll just go and fetch your tea."

I opened the letter, hoping against hope it was from the prince.

My Dearest Gwyneth,
I'm so sorry, but there was a security breach at the palace while we were gone. That, on top of everything going on with the competi-tion, is going to keep me incredibly busy. I'm afraid I really won't be able to see you for a while. There are some other issues as well. I'll explain when I can.
Why ever did we leave the SUV? I miss it, and I miss you... Not necessarily in that order.
Security measures are being increased. I know you love to bend the

*rules, but please, do as you're told. Follow the instructions to the
letter.*

*This note was a risk, but I wanted to let you know that even if I
appear too busy or distracted, my heart is with you.*

*I said it before, and I'll say it again: do not doubt me. No matter
what. I'll be thinking of you.*

Sincerely,

Your Dallas

I folded the letter up and cradled it against my chest. I
did not doubt him. But I felt weary from Tariq and Tamara's attacks and from Shaye's failure to defend me. And it
had only been a few hours, but I missed the prince.

Ugh. Feelings were seriously inconvenient.

I understood that Dallas couldn't see me. He had a role
to play. *It's a game*, I reminded myself. *They're all playing, and
so should you.*

Instead, I pulled the blankets up over my head.

I wasn't sure I was cut out for all this maneuvering. It
was literally exhausting, and I wanted nothing more than to
stay in bed and eat biscuits until the competition ended.

Another blasted knock on the door and Evangeline
stuck her pretty face into the room. "We're here with your
tea, miss. I'm afraid it's time to get up."

I groaned but did as I was told. Bria and Bettina bustled
in. Bria took my face in her hands and *tsked*. "I knew that
Tamara was going to have a fit. But you can't let her get to
you. It shows all over your face!"

She hustled off to the wardrobe to pick out a dress. She
pulled out a stunning emerald velvet gown and fingered it
approvingly. "The best revenge is looking good. You are
going to bring it today, if I have anything to do with it!"

Evangeline and Bria nodded at the dress. "That'll do the trick." Evangeline smiled at me in encouragement.

I beamed at them, in spite of wanting to hide. I loved that my maids were rooting for me to the point of revenge-dressing me for breakfast.

"How is your sister?" Bettina helped Evangeline set up the tea service. "Is she really better?"

"She is, thank you. The prince had an excellent doctor treat her, and she was given IVs, which she desperately needed. It took a couple of days, but her fever broke. You should have seen her when she met the prince. She was positively beside herself." I grinned. "She kept calling him 'Your Highness' at every opportunity. It was adorable."

"And how did the prince get on with your family?" Bria asked.

"He was wonderful. He played with my little brother, and he made Winnie feel so special. He even managed to handle my mother. It was lovely."

The twins shot each other a knowing look.

"What was that for?" I asked them.

Bria smirked. "You're gushing, my lady."

I scoffed. "I am not."

Her eyes sparkled. "Are so—and I'm so glad to hear it. The prince is worthy of gushing. And if I may say so, so are you."

She hustled to change me out of my nightgown. "So do not let the jackals get to you. Nothing can stand in the way of something that's meant to be. Nothing."

I HESITATED BEFORE ENTERING THE COMMON ROOM. I

couldn't bear to sit with Tamara and Shaye again. Tamara wasn't the worst of it. She barely concerned me. I expected her lewd speculations and jealousy. But I felt quite disappointed in Shaye, even though she hadn't really said anything. Maybe it was the fact that she *hadn't* really said anything—even in my defense—that had me feeling let down.

"Hey," a friendly voice called from behind me. "You're late, too?" Blake came even with me, a big smile on her pretty face. "Want to sit together? I know Tamara's been being a beast."

I exhaled in relief. "I'd love to. Thank you."

Shaye and Tamara watched me with thinly veiled interest as I came into the room, but I ignored them. Several of the other girls openly stared, too, but I kept my head held high as Blake and I found seats at an empty table.

"You look lovely." Blake put milk in her tea. "I kind of thought you'd go for mousy today, with all the drama, but I'm glad you didn't."

"You thought about what I'd wear today?"

Blake laughed. "We had a pool going, silly. While everybody's gossiping, I'm staying busy trying to earn a living."

"There's a pool about how I'd dress today?"

She shrugged. "It's been a bit boring without the prince. We have to keep things interesting. And plus, some of these girls have more money than they know what to do with. We aren't playing for chocolate croissants, I'll tell you. Hustling them is like taking candy from babies, although quite a bit more satisfying."

I shook my head and grabbed an enormous muffin, bursting with blueberries. "You're ridiculous."

"I'm an entrepreneur. Plus, there was no one left to

hustle in my settlement. Everyone's gone broke. This is much more fun."

I laughed, relaxing a little. But then a girl at the table next to me whispered something to her friend, and they both looked at me with disapproval.

I put down my muffin. "Everyone's talking about me. Tamara said they all think I've been...improper...with the prince."

Blake tore my muffin in half, helping herself.

"Hey!"

"Well if you're not going to eat it... I told you I was an entrepreneur. That means I'm opportunistic!"

I laughed again, but then I sighed as I caught the girls at the next table still staring. "Doesn't it bother you? Sitting with the Pageant harlot?"

"You're hardly that. Tamara was the one who'd been going around, saying that she'd like to show the prince what a *real* woman's like." She snorted. "I, for one, don't care if you get improper with the prince, so long as it's your choice. Your body, your choice, I say."

"I think the general objection is that my body's keeping the prince from everyone else's. I meant, at least from all the dates he's supposed to go on."

She shrugged. "If the prince isn't interested in someone, that's rather their problem, isn't it? Not yours. He's not interested in me, but you don't see me whinging about."

"Why is that?" I quickly buttered the other half of my muffin, lest she try and take the whole thing.

"Because I believe if something's meant to be, it's meant to be. What's the point of crying over something that's not yours? It only means it probably never will be, and it would be in your best interest to move on."

"Blake. You're smart."

"It's true. I had to drop out of school, of course, but while I was there, I always got top grades." She looked around the room, her pretty face scrunched into a frown. "While I have your ear and you're thinking I'm all smart, let me give you some more wisdom: girls can really be prats. You'll be happier if you ignore them."

I nodded, hoping I could follow her sage advice, grateful that I at least still had a friend. Shaye waved to me from her table, but I averted my eyes. Maybe I'd be better at this ignoring business than I'd thought. Feeling slightly better, I grabbed another biscuit.

WE SAT THROUGH MS. BLAKELY'S LECTURE ABOUT THE evolution of social etiquette at royal parties. The morning dragged. Shaye tried to catch my eye a couple of times, but I continued to ignore her, even though it made me feel bad. I tried to focus on the lecture, not on my friend's questionable loyalty.

At the end of the class, a royal sentinel handed Ms. Blakely a note. "Ladies," she said, "you're invited to a special screening of the newest Pageant episode. Go and see Mira in the west lounge."

Tamara managed to wedge herself next to me as we headed down the hall to the west wing. "This is going to be a good one. I guarantee it."

"Because it's starring you, beating the prince at chess and tricking him into kissing you?"

She tossed her long, raven hair and it fluttered in waves back down to her shoulders. "That, and I also had a visit from His Highness late last night." She winked at me. "This episode's sure to be a scorcher."

I balled my hands into fists, but I forced myself to smile at her. "How nice for you. I can't wait to see it." I'd rather stick a dull pencil in my eye, but no way was I going to let the little douche-whinger know *that*.

Blake gave me a thumbs-up as Tamara flounced off, chest heaving, to catch up with Shaye. "Nice work. Never let them see you sweat."

I smiled bravely, but dread pooled in my belly as we took seats in the lounge. *Dallas visited Tamara late last night?* No good could come of that. The news gave me every ick-factor in existence.

A few rows ahead, Tamara talked animatedly to the girls to her right. Shaye sat, picking at her dress, to Tamara's left. She looked uncomfortable and possibly as if she might cry. My stomach sank.

"Good morning, ladies!" Mira Kinney sang out. She was dressed to thrill in a hot-pink skirt suit and sky-high spiked heels. "I am so excited to share this episode with you. We were up all night putting it together. It includes all the recent updates, including footage of the second dates and the prince's mission trip to Settlement Four. I think the settlers are going to go wild for this episode, and you will, too. So let's roll it!"

I sat back and watched the opening sequence, trying to reel in my anxiety. The first part of the show was Tariq announcing the remaining four weeks of the contest and the news about the royal gala. There was no doubt in my mind the viewers were going to be excited about that. A fancy ball, followed by the announcement of the four finalists—the ratings were going to shoot right off the charts.

Then the footage showed the remaining twenty girls in various pursuits at the palace—having breakfast, listening to lectures, meeting with the seamstresses for fittings. The next part featured my riding date with Dallas. I shifted uncomfortably in my seat at first, worrying what the other girls might be thinking. But when I saw us riding across the lawn together at top speed, my heart soared with the memory of that day.

Dallas looked strapping and regal astride his horse. The wind whipped my braid as Maeve and I caught up to him. Then the film showed us sitting near the lake. The prince was witty, charming, and impossibly handsome as he sipped his rosé and we looked out at the view. My heart twisted. I longed to be back there with him.

The final part of the segment showed when we'd been about to kiss and the well-meaning guard had interrupted us. Dallas turned to him, his face twisted in annoyance. *"Oh, for the love of all things holy. Your timing's horrible!"*

Several of the girls chuckled at this, and the tightness in my chest eased a bit.

"After enjoying his ride with Miss West, Prince Black decided to open the stables to all of the contestants for their enjoyment," Mira Kinney said in a voice-over. There was footage of the day all the contestants had spent in the stables, laughing, talking, and brushing the horses. There was no mention that I'd been the one to ask for that particular privilege, but I didn't let it bother me.

"His Royal Highness had planned to have his next second date with Miss Tamara Layne of Settlement Eleven. But news of a tragic situation reached the palace, upending his plans. Gwyneth West's younger sister, all of seven years old, had become very ill with the flu."

They showed a picture of Winnie. I had no idea where they'd gotten it—*my mother?*

Dallas appeared on the screen, next to Mira Kinney and her microphone. "Tell me about this very serious situation," she said.

"We weren't sure if Miss West's sister was going to make it." He looked quite serious. "But my family wanted to help in any way we could. We sent our best doctor to Settlement Four to help save this little girl. Thankfully, we were able to get there in time."

"And you offered to bring Miss West home to see her sister?" Mira asked.

"Yes. I knew that, if I were in Miss West's situation, I would want the opportunity to go home and see my family. I wanted to offer that to her."

"That was *very* generous of you," Mira gushed.

Dallas shook his head. "It was the right thing to do. When you think of it that way, it's really quite simple."

The next footage was of the two of us in my neighborhood and then a brief interview with my sister. She'd had some makeup put on, and her hair was fixed very cutely. "I'm feeling so much better," she said, her little voice just about breaking my heart, "because of the prince. His Highness came here to save me, and he brought my sister to visit. It made me feel so much better." She smiled broadly for the camera.

A lot of girls in the audience said, "aw." More than one put a hand over her heart, as if Winnie had given them all the feels.

The next shot was of us driving away from my neighborhood with the prince smiling broadly and waving to all the civilians. They'd even captured the young girl sitting on her father's shoulders, squealing with delight when Dallas waved to her.

Mira's narrative continued. "His Highness was delighted to have the opportunity to travel to Settlement Four. He hopes to pay many more visits to all of the settlements in the near future. He's a leader who truly loves his people."

The next image was of the prince and me returning to the castle. I was relieved to see I didn't look as bad as I'd thought. There was no visual evidence that Dallas and I had been snogging like crazy in the car. He leaned over and kissed me, and my heart swelled. Even though it wasn't *our* kiss, it was still sweet and tender. I thought I heard several of the other girls sigh, and I wondered if they hated me.

"That was brilliant," Blake whispered to me. "You didn't come off like a harlot at all. You seemed quite pious, with your sick sister and all."

I giggled in spite of myself. "Thanks."

"Returning to his many duties as prince, His Highness still made time to have a second date with Miss Layne upon his return to the castle." The footage showed Dallas and Tamara playing chess. She laughed at something he said, her bust straining against the tight fabric of her dress. That hadn't been the order of things—Dallas had gone on his date with Tamara before he'd taken me home—but I chalked it up to artistic license.

But then they took it a bit further. "If I win, you will honor me with a kiss," Dallas said in a voice-over as it showed him taking Tamara's queen.

What the what?

Tamara looked back at me, tossing her hair over her shoulder. She gave me a wicked grin.

It showed him winning the match and smiling broadly. The next image was the two them standing close together.

The prince leaned over Tamara and she fastened her hands at the base of his neck, just like he'd shown me.

But the kiss he gave her was *not* chaste, and it was not merely "kiss-ish," as he'd described it. His hands roamed down her back as she clung to him.

The kiss deepened and she moaned. I clutched my stomach, feeling sick.

"Miss Layne," Dallas said, pulling back, "you are quite something."

She beamed up at him, biting her lip. "Your Highness. Don't make me blush."

I squirmed uncomfortably in my seat as they eye-snogged each other.

The footage cut to a stately home in a beautiful neighborhood. Mira Kinney narrated, "Miss Layne hails from Settlement Eleven, where her parents are active in community and cultural outreach programs."

They showed more scenes from Settlement 11, including two good-looking, well-dressed adults who must be Tamara's parents. "Mr. and Mrs. Layne, long-time supporters of the royal family, are beacons in Settlement Eleven. They serve on multiple boards, many of which focus on underprivileged children in at-risk home environments."

"That's code for 'they have money up to their eyeballs,'" Blake whispered.

I nodded. It was all I could manage. I'd been rendered speechless.

The episode came back to Mira Kinney, who sat in an overstuffed chair in one of the castle's formal rooms. "As you can tell, Settlers, things are heating up in the Pageant. His Royal Highness is going to have some difficult choices to make over the next few weeks."

She smiled at the cameras, but a chill went down my spine as two pictures appeared on the screen. In the upper left corner, there was a picture of me from the night of my first date with the prince. I wore the gorgeous red gown my maids had chosen. In the upper right corner, there was a shot of Tamara, all curves and a killer smile in her low-cut teal gown she'd worn on *her* first date with the prince.

Mira kept up her dazzling smile. "On the one hand, he has Miss Gwyneth West, hailing from a modest home in Settlement Four. Miss West is clearly dedicated to her family and loves animals." They showed footage of me brushing Maeve, a large, goofy smile on my face. They showed Dallas kissing me again, which in contrast to the tonsil-hockey he'd played with Tamara, looked positively platonic.

"On the other hand," Mira continued, "there's Miss Layne, whose sophistication and ravishing personality are clearly difficult for His Highness to ignore." The footage was of them kissing again, and I vowed to go and pummel every person in the camera crew, right down to the last production assistant, one by one—right after I pummeled Tamara and Dallas, not necessarily in that order.

The image returned to Mira herself, all smiles—the cat who'd invited all the canaries to come and play. "Not to mention, His Highness has many more first and second dates to go on, with eighteen other beautiful, talented, and intelligent young women. All of this will culminate in a royal gala, at which the four finalists will be announced."

Mira beamed at the camera. "I don't know about you, but I cannot *wait* to find out what happens. The excitement here at the palace is palpable. So stay tuned for the next episodes, and see who the prince chooses to propose to! I can promise you, I'm on pins and needles right there with you. It appears we've got a real contest going!"

She smiled one last time for the camera. "Can't wait to watch the next episode and find out what happens next."

You could tell, unequivocally, that she meant it.

CHAPTER 19
ONE LONELY STAR

SHAYE WAITED FOR ME IN THE HALL. I TRIED TO ZIGZAG through the other girls to avoid her, but she caught up to me. "Gwyneth, a word." She sighed. "Please."

"Fine." I didn't want to talk to her, but it was better than getting stuck near Tamara, who was bragging loudly about the prince's kissing abilities and what the size of his hands suggested about the rest of him.

"Let's go outside," Shaye suggested.

But a guard blocked the door to the eastern grounds. "You may go out, my ladies," he said, "but only with security."

He motioned to two nearby sentinels. "Accompany the ladies out on the grounds."

The four of us stepped outside, but the guards hung back a bit. At least they were giving us some room to talk. I side-eyed Shaye and sighed, suddenly wishing they were crowding us. I wasn't sure I was ready to hear whatever she had to say.

"I'm sorry I didn't stick up for you more." She gave me a

miserable look. "But Tamara had been beating me down relentlessly, insisting that you and the prince were being inappropriate."

"I can't believe you listened to her!" I cried.

"I didn't." She shook her head. "I mean, I did because she's *loud*, and she doesn't stop talking, but I never believed what she said."

I shrugged. "It's fine. And the irony of it is, Tamara would be the first one to brag about riding The Royal Stallion. She was just trying to turn everyone against me."

"True." Shaye watched the stone pavement as we walked. "I wouldn't even care if you were getting special treatment in exchange for something. I'd just be worried about you."

I put my hand on my hip. "I know it's hard to believe that His Highness actually likes me for me, not for any other reason, but it's true. At least, I thought it was." I shook my head, as if I could dislodge the images of him kissing Tamara.

"Of course he does." Shaye finally looked at me. "I think I was just letting jealousy get the best of me. I really am sorry. I wasn't being a good friend."

I sighed. Any trace of anger I'd been holding onto dissipated. "I'd love to say I had no idea what you meant because I was above being jealous, but of course I do. I acted like a cow after I saw your episode."

She laughed a little. "It can be hard to watch."

"I owe you an apology, too."

Shaye smiled. "I accept. And speaking of episodes, you did very well in yours."

"They edited it so it barely resembled real life."

"I know. The part with Tamara and the prince kissing?"

She leaned closer, conspiratorially. "They filmed that last night. Her maids got her out of bed and had her put on the same dress, the one she'd worn when they played chess. Tariq arranged the whole thing. She said they had to do several takes."

My temper rose. "Several takes of them all over each other?"

Shaye nodded. "Tariq told them he wanted the kiss to be more dramatic."

"And the prince did as he was told."

"Don't be too hard on him. I'm sure he didn't enjoy it."

I scoffed. "It's not as though he were kissing a blob fish."

Shaye started laughing, and even though my blood was practically boiling, I joined her.

"I don't know what a blob fish is, but yeah, I get your point."

I stopped laughing. "I don't know what to do."

Shaye linked her arm through mine. "You have to ignore it. Otherwise, the next few weeks will tear you up."

"I don't know if I *can* ignore it."

"But you have to learn to deal with the un-pleasantries," Shaye said. "If you were to become the princess, can you imagine how much more you'd have to deal with than all this?"

"I wouldn't have to deal with Tamara's boobs in the prince's face," I quipped.

Shaye bit her lip. She seemed to choose her words carefully. "It might not be Tamara, but the prince is in a position of unparalleled power. He is also handsome and charming. Someone will always be shoving their boobs in his face, I'm afraid"

I stopped walking. "That's not very encouraging."

Shaye tilted her head, inspecting me. "I was not being a good friend yesterday. Today, I am trying to make that right."

"By scaring me?"

"By telling you the truth. If you think the competition's intense, imagine what being a royal would really be like. You'd have a new family to navigate—which is a whole new world, really, filled with vampires—and then you have the political side of it, not to mention a new husband and a large household to run—all of the other tasks that would consume a young princess."

My jaw dropped. "Are you trying to talk me out of the competition?"

"No. Absolutely not." Shaye smiled, surprising me. "These are the things I remind myself of when I'm confronted by the fact that the prince seems to vastly prefer you. But I also think they're real and that you should be aware of them. Do not let Tamara's heaving bosom distract you from the competition. And be sure that if you beat her, it's because you really want to win."

We walked in silence for a moment, circling the reflecting pools. "Do you want to win?" I finally asked.

Shaye shrugged. "I thought I did. I'm certainly not ready to go back to my muddy little village. But when it comes to the prince and all the trouble surrounding the palace, I don't know what I think."

"Did you hear about the rebel who escaped?" I hadn't mentioned a word to anyone, but Shaye usually heard about these things from her maids.

"Yes, I did. And that's exactly the sort of trouble I'm talking about. I don't know if it's *safe* to be a princess. Who knows what the rebels have planned?"

I nodded. "It's scary to think about."

"Much scarier than Tamara," Shaye agreed, "and that's saying something."

I GLIMPSED DALLAS WITH THE KING LATER THAT afternoon. They were talking in hushed tones with one of their advisors.

He caught sight of me, and our gazes locked for a moment. I felt that pull toward him, an undertow threatening to take me under.

He nodded curtly then strode off with the king and the other man. He didn't give me a backward glance.

Do not doubt me. His words rang in my ears. But as I watched him disappear down the hall, my heart still twisted. *He's trying to protect you from the king,* I reminded myself.

An image with his tongue jammed down Tamara's throat flashed in my mind. I shook my head, as if to clear it. I refused to doubt him. And yet, a tiny part of me worried. That current, the torrent of feeling coursing through me, felt dangerous. If I gave into it and let it take me under... And if he wasn't there to meet me, waiting back at the shore...

I might never recover from this. So I did not doubt him. But in that moment, I started to doubt myself.

CHAPTER 20
HANGING ON

"YOU HAVE A LETTER," EVANGELINE SAID.

"Thank you." I hadn't heard news from home for a few days. Hoping it was from my mother with an update on Winnie, I opened it eagerly.

Dear Gwyneth,

I hope you are well and that your travels were not too exhausting. I'm writing to tell you that your sister is much improved. She got up and played with her dolls for several hours today. It was the longest she'd been off the couch. Her color is returning, as is her appetite, all thanks to the prince.

I hope you know how much I appreciate that you came here to help us. Also, our last words have been troubling me. I do not want you to think that I'm burdening you with too much responsibility or that I don't have faith because I do, absolutely, have faith in you. Since your father and Balkyn have been gone, you have helped me run the household and care for your brother and sister. I know you are more than a selfish girl.

I might have spoken too harshly—but I see that the prince is within

*your grasp, and you might not. It was amazing to experience the
transformation that his power can bring. He saved your sister's life,
and he did it because he favors you.*

*That sort of power should not be ignored. Think of all the good you
could do if the crown was yours. Not to needle you, my love, but I
am your mother. It's my job.*

Please tell the prince we send our warm thanks and kindest regards.
Love,
Mom

I snorted when I put the letter down. *No pressure or
anything, Mom.* But of course, she was right. The prince's
power should not be ignored, in particular, the power he
had over me.

Head muddled with competing thoughts, I hurried to
get dressed.

❦

SHAYE CAME AND SAT WITH BLAKE AND ME AT BREAKFAST.
"I don't know if I can handle Tamara any more," she
moaned.

"I heard that." Tamara plopped herself down next to
her, grinning madly. "And I refuse to get worked up
about it."

"Because you were already too worked up by the prince,
and you've got nothing left?" Blake asked, clearly joking.

"Ha,ha." Still, Tamara looked like a cat who'd just been
served cream. "The prince sent me flowers this morning.
Just look at the card!"

Dear Miss Layne,
Thank you for your kind attention during our date and all the post-
production work we had to do. I appreciate your patience with me
more than you know.
The episode turned out well. My father was very pleased with it.
Look forward to beating you at chess again soon.
Sincerely,
Prince Black

I nearly spit my tea out. *My father was very pleased...* That did not bode well for me—not at all.

"I don't know what you're so excited about," I said meanly. "'Post-production work?' It sounds like he's talking about tuning up a car."

"Now who's the jealous cow?" Tamara smiled at me merrily.

"I'm not jealous." The lie was feeble at best.

Do not doubt me. I heard it again.

Then do not behave like a jackass, I thought back.

Tariq zipped over to our table, beaming. "I just heard about the flowers. Congratulations, Tamara."

"It feels good to be the front runner." She shot him a megawatt smile. "I'm just hoping these other girls can keep up, so the show doesn't get boring too fast. We need to keep those ratings up!"

"Things are never boring when you're about." He smiled at her indulgently. "But speaking of the other girls, Blake my dear, you have a first date tonight. Shaye, you have a second this afternoon."

"Today?" Shaye spluttered.

"Yes." Tariq looked her up and down. "You might want

to address your hair. Ladies." Always in a self-important rush, he turned on his heel and was gone.

Shaye examined her hair, perplexed, as Blake pushed the pancakes around on her plate.

"What's the matter with you?" Tamara snapped.

"Nothing." Blake blinked at us. "But what on earth am I going to talk to him about?"

"If you ask Tamara," Shaye said, tucking a curl behind her ear, "she'll tell you talking's overrated."

Tamara rolled her eyes then turned to Blake. She looked at her as if seeing her for the first time, perhaps recognizing Blake's beauty and viewing her as a threat. "You should talk about your hair and how you do your makeup. Ooh, and about your period. Tell him all about your menstrual cycle. Men love that sort of talk."

"No they don't." Blake scoffed. "I have a brother. He likes talking about farts."

Tamara shrugged, dismissing her. "So talk about farting then, and see how far that gets you." She got a dreamy look on her face. "It doesn't matter anyway. He sent me flowers. He only has eyes—and lips, might I remind you—for me."

Oh, sure, you squat-loving douche-nozzle.

But I said nothing, forcing myself to enjoy my pancakes instead. I was making myself look on the bright side, but it wasn't easy because sitting here, listening to Tamara go on and on about her relationship with Dallas, I was starting to feel as if I was going a bit crazy.

Was it only a few days ago that we'd visited my sister, that Dallas had held me in his arms? It seemed as though centuries had passed. And seeing him in the hall like that, cool and distant, had only made me feel more schizophrenic.

It's the contest. It's the game. It's political. Still, I felt disjointed, as if all of my pieces weren't adding up.

Maybe if I told my friends the truth, it'd make me feel better, more whole. But even though I could have bragged, and talked about the moments the prince and I had shared, I wouldn't do that. Those moments were private, for him and for me. In addition, it would hurt the other girls' feelings. I might be a jerk sometimes, but that was when my temper got the better of me. I would never do that on purpose.

But Tamara would. I watched her as she continued chatting—about her favorite topic, herself—occasionally popping a grape into her mouth. I remembered everything Dallas had said about her and how he claimed that he could never care for her.

I'd believed him. I still wanted to believe him. But if he'd told the truth, what on earth was he playing at now?

TARIQ PULLED ME ASIDE AFTER OUR MORNING LESSONS. "Miss West. I need to speak with you, please."

"Oh joy, your Royal Emissary."

He frowned, then ushered me into the library. "I have a favor to ask."

"Like I said, joy." I knew he'd do this sooner or later. It just happened to be sooner than I'd like.

"I want to film a scene with you and the prince this afternoon."

"But you said he had a date with Shaye and then one with Blake."

"He does." Tariq clasped his hands together. "But that is

none of your concern. I've sent a special dress to your maids. Put it on after lunch. I'll send for you when we're ready."

"But what do you want me to—"

His eyes flashed in annoyance. "As I said, it's none of your concern. The production crew and I are handling everything. See you in a bit." He hustled off before I could finish my question or object. As I watched his retreating form, I felt certain that's exactly the way he wanted it.

CHAPTER 21
FIRE I CAN SPARK

"THAT'S THE DRESS?" I TOOK A STEP BACK FROM THE offensive garment.

"It's not that bad." Bria fingered the sequins. "It's just a bit...leggy."

I eyed the gown, what there was of it. It was black sequined with a halter neck, an open back, and a slit in the front that would practically go up to my eyeballs.

I crossed my arms against my chest. "No way."

Evangeline sighed. "I'm afraid the royal emissary insisted. He told me to remind you that you owe him a favor." She wrinkled her nose. "I highly doubted it, but you know how he can be. No use arguing with that one."

"I'm sorry you had to deal with him." I was even sorrier I'd agreed to do as he asked.

"Well, there's no time like the present." Bettina hauled out the makeup crate. "Let's get to work."

I sighed as Bria started in on my hair. "So this dress... Does that mean you have another date with the prince, so soon?" she asked.

"That's the thing—no, I don't. So what are they planning for me?"

My maids looked at each other, clearly perplexed.

But I was almost glad that no one had an answer. I was pretty sure that I didn't want to know.

❦

I TEETERED DOWN THE STAIRS IN MY HEELS. THE DRESS'S front slit had one upside—I could freely take a step. Still, I cursed under my breath as I cautiously descended, praying I didn't trip. The last thing I needed was to break my neck and bleed out while surrounded by vampires.

Tariq met me in the grand foyer. He beamed when he saw me. "You look perfect."

"I look ridiculous."

"I should've expected you'd be difficult." He rolled his eyes. "Follow me."

Eve passed us in the hall. "Where are you going, dressed like that? You look like a human sacrifice!"

I sighed. "Something for the Pageant."

Tariq grunted, impatient as ever. "Enough, ladies. Gwyneth, we're on a schedule."

I clasped Eve's hand as I passed, wishing I could stay and talk with her. "I'll come and see you soon." Not only did I want to avoid whatever it was Tariq had planned for me, I needed her. Eve was a great reality check. She could probably talk me down from the ledge I felt myself fast approaching.

"I can't wait to catch up and hear what this," she pointed at my dress, "is all about. His Highness is going to lose it when he sees you."

"We'll see," I said weakly. Feeling that something was absolutely going to be lost—most likely my dignity—I followed Tariq with slumped shoulders.

"Posture, Gwyneth, posture."

I straightened up, giving him side-eye a safe distance behind his back.

We arrived at one of the formal lounges, and he peered inside. "Ah, Mira's ready for us."

"Are you putting me on camera right this instant?"

He smiled with what looked like feigned patience. "No, we're going to brief you first. But don't smudge your makeup because you're going on soon."

He ushered me inside, and Mira waved us over. She'd set up at one of the tables with her notes spread everywhere. Her assistant, Rose, paced nearby. She kept reviewing things on her clipboard and muttering to herself.

"Don't mind Rose." Mira motioned for us to take seats. "She's just trying to figure out the final dating slots. With the prince's busy schedule, it's a nightmare. Thank goodness, we're in the home stretch."

She smiled at me. "You're looking very sharp, Gwyneth."

I frowned. "My vampire friend just told me I looked like a human sacrifice."

Mira laughed politely. "Well, your friend's not entirely wrong."

"I'm sorry?" I spluttered.

"No, no, don't misunderstand me. It's just that Tariq's raised some concerns about your...presentation...in the show, and he's asked us to address it."

"I don't understand."

Mira's gaze flicked to Tariq then back to me. "After the last episode, he's concerned that you're coming off as too vanilla. I thought it would work, casting you as the good girl and Tamara as the vixen, but Tariq's worried that you're falling a bit flat. And after doing some polling, I can't disagree with him."

"So you wanted to change my look to *this*?" I picked at the flimsy gown. "Even Tamara wouldn't wear this dress!"

"Sure, she would." Mira chuckled. "Now, we're going to give you some lines. It's not a script, per se, but a suggestion about what to say in your scene."

I blinked at her. "You're staging this."

Mira and Tariq exchanged a look. "It's more like we're putting an editorial spin on it."

"I don't want to do it." I'd liked Mira up to this point, but what she was proposing didn't sit well with me. "I feel like it's lying. This is supposed to be a reality show."

Mira smiled tightly. "Here are the lines. Why don't you read them and take a moment, while I check in with Rose?" She handed me a piece of paper and excused herself.

I read the script. I put the paper back on the table. "There's no way in hell I'm saying that."

"Why, Gwyneth, of course there is," Tariq said silkily. "I've only just come from a meeting with the king. He was ranting and raving about the rebels and how we need to control the situation."

"Did something happen?"

"There's been hints of another upcoming attack on the palace," Tariq said. The self-satisfied tone dropped from his voice, and he became all business. "The king's reasonably upset."

I shook my head. "I don't understand what any of this has to do with me or the Pageant."

"I'm worried that the king thinks the contest is

contributing to the rebel attacks. With the increased publicity surrounding the Pageant, the rebels have become bolder. It's like they're trying to take advantage of the spotlight. The king has raised the question if it's safe to continue."

"That's one thing." I bit my lip. "But can you explain to me why, because of the rebels, you want me interrupt the prince's date and say this garbage? What does any of this have to do with me?"

Tariq sighed. "The king also said, and this is a quote— that no son of his 'was going to be involved with rebel scum.'"

My cheeks heated. "And you're insinuating that he was talking about me?"

"Of course he was. You're the one who let Benjamin Vale out of his cage. It's not like the king has forgotten about it." Tariq picked up the piece of paper and jabbed his finger at it. "You see, I'm trying to protect you with this just like the prince has tried to protect you from his father."

"You're trying to make me look bad in front of the prince, his father, and everyone else in the settlements."

"My goal is to have it look as if you and the prince are at odds. If things have cooled between you, the king will not see you as a threat. He won't make a fuss, and the contest can continue, unfettered."

I scoffed. "But Mira just said I'm too 'vanilla.' So I'm not a threat, anyway!"

Tariq tilted his head, inspecting me. "The latest polls say you're the Pageant's front runner by a mile."

"Oh." I never would've expected that. "So Mira just lied to me about the polling?"

"She presented facts strategically in order to persuade

you. That's not lying. I didn't want to get into all of this if
we could avoid it."

I rubbed my temples. All of these maneuverings were
mixing together, spinning out beyond my comprehension.

"Gwyneth." He waited until I looked at him, then he
continued. "With this latest update on the rebels and the
fear of another rebel attack, I'm worried that the king is
going to clean house. After what happened with Benjamin
Vale, you're vulnerable. If he believes the prince still has a
strong attachment to you, he will view you as a potential
weakness, and he will have you sent home."

"Wouldn't that suit you fine? You said you wanted me to
go rot back in Four. Then you and Tamara can plan the
wedding of the century, while I eat beans from a tin for the
rest of my life."

"I would certainly enjoy that." He sighed. "But after
spending time with the prince this week and seeing him
with Tamara and the other contestants, I'm afraid those
dreams of mine are in direct opposition with reality. He's
putting on a show for the cameras while he bides his time,
waiting for the end of the contest. That's all."

I felt a headache coming on. *Was he telling the truth?* "So?"

"So I'm worried that the prince is going to try and
throw the contest if the king kicks you out." Tariq let that
sink in.

"Do you really think that's going to happen?"

"You know that His Highness is stubborn and strong-
willed. The king is just as bad, if not worse." Tariq's nostrils
flared. "The Pageant is my baby, and it *will* succeed. I will
not see it undone because of a royal pissing contest."

"But by saying these things, I am going to hurt the
prince."

"You will hurt him in the short term," Tariq acknowledged. "In the long term, you will save him from himself and from the king. You will save him by saving yourself."

I snatched the piece of paper from him. "After this, the king will hate me even more. I'll look the fool."

"The king will no longer see you as a threat, and that's a good thing. Flying under the radar for the rest of the competition is in your best interest. He will no longer think you have the prince's favor, and you will no longer concern him."

"And what if it's true, that I no longer have the prince's favor? And what about the godforsaken polls you are all so concerned with?"

"I can't control the prince's feelings. And maybe you can't, either." Tariq's eyes glittered. "As for the polls, the viewers love a good drama. They'll be rooting for you. I know it."

"So you are doing this to...help me?"

Tariq chuckled. "Make no mistake, Gwyneth. I'm only interested in helping myself."

"Ah. I see." Because I finally did.

Mira came back to her desk. "Are we ready?" She sounded quite sure that the answer would be yes.

But all I wanted to say was *no*.

CHAPTER 22
GAMES

GOOSEBUMPS BROKE OUT ALL OVER MY ARMS AS I WAITED in the wings. "This feels wrong," I whispered to Tariq.

"Put your feelings to the side. Remember what matters most: the prince."

I shot him a look. His pretty face was half-framed in shadow. If there was anyone I shouldn't trust, it was Tariq. And yet, the prince *was* what mattered most to me. I had to protect him, even if it meant hurting him—and hurting myself—not to mention Shaye. I hadn't really given that a lot of thought, but as I peered at her, sitting with the prince and laughing, I realized that she was going to be more than a little upset. I was about to rain on her parade. Pour on it, actually.

Mira bustled in. "It's time. They're just finishing their game."

"Why are all the second dates about games?" I asked.

"It's because of security concerns. The Black Guard doesn't want the prince roaming too far because of the prisoner who escaped."

I nodded, watching as Dallas and Shaye flipped up numbers on the board game they were playing. Dallas rolled the dice, and Shaye clapped, cheering him on.

Mira turned to me, smoothing my hair and adjusting my gown. "I know you don't like that dress, but it's becoming."

"I don't want to do it," I said again.

"I know." Mira smiled at me kindly. "Do your best. There's a good reason for it, right?"

My gaze wandered over to Tariq, who watched Shaye and Dallas with interest. "I hope so."

Mira leaned forward and whispered in my ear. "I'm rooting for you. I won't make you look bad in the final cut, I promise. I've been doing this for a long time. This scene will be good for ratings, I promise. Everyone loves a good conflict."

"What's that?" Tariq asked.

"Nothing," Mira said. "I was just giving Gwyneth a little friendly female advice."

"Right. Is it time?" Tariq gave me another once-over. "She looks ready."

"We can send her in now." Mira nodded at me. "Go ahead, Gwyneth. The sooner you start, the sooner you'll be finished."

I nodded, teetering on my heels. I could hear the blood rushing in my ears as I went through the door without knocking. The cameras swung in my direction.

"Your Highness." My voice came out hoarse. "A word."

Dallas looked up from the game, completely taken aback, and the smile disappeared from his face. He shot to his feet. "Gwyneth? What's the matter?"

"I need to talk to you." I barely got the words out. My mouth had gone completely dry.

Shaye looked at me, worry plain on her face. "Are you all right? Is it your sister?"

Her kind concern just made this worse. I took a step forward, remembering my instructions. "My sister's fine. I just wanted to see His Highness."

They looked at each other quickly, confused.

Shaye laughed nervously. "Well, His Highness is sort of on a date right now."

"I don't care." I stepped forward again, a bit recklessly.

Dallas finally noticed my dress and all the makeup. He looked concerned. "Miss West, are you quite all right? You don't seem yourself."

"I just—I just wanted to see you." That, at least, was the truth.

He looked at Shaye. "Would you mind giving us a moment?" He sounded uncomfortable.

Her mouth briefly puckered in annoyance, but then she nodded, ever the peacemaker. She swiftly left the room, mercifully without giving me a backward glance.

Dallas immediately came to my side. "Gwyneth, what's wrong?"

"I haven't seen you all week." My voice wobbled. This was part of the script, but I felt the words sharply. And I hated myself for it.

He reached for my hand. "I know. I'm sorry, but I've been busy."

"I k-know. But I had to see you. I'm tired of waiting. I'm tired of you spending time with these other girls." My eyes pricked with tears. The tears were not scripted.

He turned back to the cameraman. "Can you stop filming?"

The cameraman shook his head no then made the sign for *still rolling*.

Dallas turned back to me, annoyed—whether with the cameraman or me, I wasn't sure. "Can we please talk about this later? I'll figure out a way we can meet in private." He kept his voice low.

"I don't want to wait." I wanted to get out of here, away from the cameras, away from Tariq and Mira Kinney watching me from the next room.

"Tell me what's wrong." He rubbed the back of my hand with his thumb.

"I saw you with Tamara again, and I know you sent her flowers." My voice was flat, dead. "I saw you kiss her."

He sighed deeply, shooting a quick glance back toward the cameras. "That's complicated."

I hoped that was code for 'I didn't want to do it but the network insisted,' but of course, I didn't dare ask. Instead, I took a step closer.

Dallas's eyes raked over my dress, and the muscle in his jaw jumped. "What are you doing?"

"Coming closer. Like I said, I missed you." In a move I'd cribbed from Tamara, I stuck my chest out a bit.

Dallas's gaze darkened, and he frowned. "Gwyneth. I'm with Shaye tonight. Shaye's your friend." He spoke to me as if he were trying to wake me from a trance.

"I don't care." They'd written that for me, too—banking on the fact that the prince would be the perfect gentleman —but I would've said it anyway. I hated having him so close, but not being able to touch him, to show him how I truly felt, to claim him.

I hated having to politely wait in line. I felt my temper

rising. I reached out and stroked his cheek, and he winced. "Please. You're not yourself tonight."

"You don't want me?" I asked hoarsely.

His face crumbled. "That's not fair. You're putting me in an impossible situation."

"That makes two of us," I whispered. Those words were my own, unscripted.

Shaye poked her head back into the room. "Are you quite finished?"

Dallas and I stared at each other, and I nodded. "Yes. I believe we are."

He stepped back, as if I'd struck him. "My lady."

"Your Highness." I turned on my high heel and strode out, without so much as twisting my ankle. All that twisted was my heart.

CHAPTER 23
SAVE YOURSELF

"My lady, you don't have permission to go to the stables—"

"Then come with me, and watch my every move because I am going out there. Now." I brushed past the sentinel through the doors.

He cursed, but at least he followed me.

"Thank you."

I sighed in relief as we reached the large, white barn and sprawling stable. I'd missed the horses, and the peace and tranquility of this place was just what I needed after yesterday's disaster.

I'd cried myself to sleep, again. And Evangeline had pretended not to notice, again.

"I'll wait out here," the sentinel said at the stable doors. "But you mustn't stay too long, my lady. They're being very strict about the rules. You don't want to get into trouble."

"I'll just be a few minutes. I need to check on the horses." In fact, they were most likely better than I was, but I needed to see them for mental health reasons. Inside the barn, I stopped and spoke to each horse. I patted each of their soft coats, slipping them the sugar cubes and carrots I'd snuck from the kitchen.

I hadn't been able to drag myself to the common room this morning for breakfast. I knew Shaye would be upset about what I'd done, and I couldn't blame her. That didn't mean I wanted to face her.

I finally reached Maeve, and she whinnied in recognition. "Hello, my friend. There's a good girl." I gave her a carrot. "I've missed you, you know. I'd take you out riding, but everyone at the castle is being a bit cautious so no riding for us. We're like prisoners, I tell you." I gave her a sugar cube in consolation.

"Your Highness! Please!" I heard shouts from outside the stable. "That is *excessive*, Your Highness. Ow!"

Dallas strode inside, his face set with a grim fury.

He dragged a squawking Tariq behind him.

The prince dropped him onto the ground and Tariq looked up at him, seething. "Quite unnecessary, Your Highness." He struggled to his feet and dusted off his clothes to the best of his ability. "I said I'd come willingly."

"Do. Not. Speak. Unless spoken to," Dallas bit out. He turned to me, eyes blazing. "The royal emissary and I have just spoken about your performance during my date with Shaye."

I clung to Maeve. "Oh?"

"My intelligence indicates that the royal emissary chose that dress for you and sent you on the mission to interrupt my date." Dallas's nostrils flared. "Is it true?"

I looked at Tariq, not knowing what to say. If I admitted the truth, did that mean Tariq would run to the king?

"I... Uh..."

"Are you worried about him?" Dallas pointed, a bit wildly, at Tariq. "Don't be. He won't be whinging off to my father any time soon."

"I might have spoken with him about it," I finally admitted. When Tariq didn't flinch, I grew bolder. "And he totally picked out that dress."

Dallas grabbed Tariq by the ear, and the smaller man cried out in pain. "Do. Not. Ever. Pick out a dress for Miss West again."

"Yes, Your Highness," he squeaked.

Dallas released him, but anger still rolled off him in waves. "I'd have you both know something. I do not appreciate being manipulated under any circumstances."

"Your Highness," Tariq said, "the king has voiced concerns about Miss West—"

"And I have spoken to him in return," Dallas said, his voice now deadly calm. "I do not need, or want, you meddling in my family business, Tariq. It is called family business for a reason. You are an important member of our staff, but you must learn to butt out. When you try to insert yourself where you don't belong, you make a mess of things, as you did yesterday."

Tariq's brow furrowed. "My apologies, Your Highness. I thought I was helping both you and Miss West."

"That deserves a more convoluted explanation than I care to hear." He pointed to the door. "Go. And if you ever instruct the camera crew to ignore my request to stop filming again, I will have your head on a spike."

"Yes, Your Highness." With a formal bow to both of us —and no trace of irony whatsoever—Tariq fled the stable.

"Now you." Dallas's gaze burned into mine. "What on

earth were you playing at, listening to Tariq and making a fool out of both of us?"

I still clung to Maeve, hoping she'd give me strength. "He said he was worried about you. And about me. And the rebels."

Dallas frowned. "Explain."

"Tariq said that the king did not approve of me, because of my history with the rebels and Benjamin Vale. He said the king would send me home, and then you would cancel the competition, and that basically, the whole world would come crashing down if I didn't crash your date with Shaye, have you reject me, and make it seem as if there was some distance between us." I scrubbed a hand across my face. "At least, those are the parts I understood."

Dallas shook his head. He suddenly looked weary. "I'm worried about you, Gwyneth."

"What do you mean?"

"I'm worried about your judgment. You should have come to me with your concerns, instead of blindly following Tariq's scheme."

"Tariq said he'd tell the king you'd been protecting me. He threatened me."

Dallas cursed. "I'll have his head on a spike yet."

"Don't. He's not all bad." *Just a large chunk of him.*

He raked a hand through his hair. "But there's another problem here, a more vexing one. You've let these people bully you—Tariq, Tamara. You've let your emotions run away with you when you saw the episode with Shaye."

I stiffened. "I am human, you know."

Dallas cursed. "Yes, I'm aware. But you need to be strong, Gwyneth. Solid. If you want to be in this world, you have to keep your game face on, put people in their place, and stand up for yourself. Instead, you've been manipulated. You went along with a plot you didn't author."

"And you never do that." Sarcasm dripped in my voice.

"I told you before, I have a role to play." He understood me perfectly. "The contest has to seem fair."

"Is jamming your tongue down Tamara's throat necessary for fairness? Or is it something else?" Again, my temper was getting the best of me.

"They asked me to do that, to add drama to the competition." His eyes flashed. "I want *many* things, Gwyneth. One of them is for this contest to be fair, so that the people in the settlements are not disappointed. I wanted this to be a good thing, for the good of the people. The settlements' future depends on it."

"I understand." I tried to calm down before the moment got away from me. "But it's still hard to watch. And then I haven't been able to talk to you... I felt like I was going crazy..."

"I told you it would be like this, for now." Dallas looked sad. "I also told you not to doubt me."

"I didn't." But it sounded like a lie, even to me.

"I suppose I was asking too much. I am sure that, were the tables turned, I would be jealous. I would have a hard time watching you with other suitors." He tapped me under the chin, so that my gaze came level with his. "But I would give you the benefit of the doubt. At least, I hope I would."

"Dallas—"

"I have to get back to the palace." He sounded cold, distant, even though he was touching me. "I am sorry this happened and that Tariq used you in this way."

"I did it for you. I wanted to protect you."

He stroked my face, and then released me. "I did not need your protection, Gwyneth. I needed your trust."

And with that, he was gone.

CHAPTER 24
BOTH SIDES NOW

I HELD THE REINS TIGHTLY.

"Where are you going?" the sentinel bellowed.

"I'll be back soon. Don't wait for me. If anyone asks, you never saw me. I don't want to bring you any trouble." I'd done enough damage. I didn't need to drag the hapless guard down with me.

I urged Maeve on, desperate to get away from him, from everyone, from the palace. Apparently as eager as me, the mare took off. The ground flew beneath us, and the wind whipped the hair off my face. Finally, there was some distance between me and the castle. I only wished I could get away from the look of disappointment on Dallas's face. But it was branded in my memory, destined to haunt me for all of eternity.

I cursed him.

I would give you the benefit of the doubt.

Well, wasn't that just perfect? The morally and ethically immaculate prince would have handled the situation better than me if he'd been in my shoes. Must be nice. Must be nice to be so sure of everything, especially yourself.

Let him be perfect then. Maybe he would pick Shaye as his bride. They could be gorgeous and perfect and kind and morally superior together, preparing nutritious meals for peasants while looking like fashion models and just generally making anyone less perfect—i.e., everyone else—want to hurl themselves from the nearest bridge.

I grimaced. I didn't want to think about him anymore. He was through with me.

And you're through with him, I promptly reminded myself.

But still, his words were like a knife slicing through my heart. *I needed your trust.*

Pretending to myself that it was because of the wind, I let my tears freely fall.

☙❧

I DIDN'T REALIZE I'D RIDDEN BACK TO THE SPOT DALLAS had shown me, but I found myself there some time later. I tied Maeve to a tree and gave her another carrot. "Good girl." I petted her behind the ears.

She whinnied, as if she were worried about me as I started down the path. "It's okay, Maeve. I'll just be a minute."

But each step I took, I felt more weighted down with dread. I couldn't stop the flood of memories. The day that Dallas had brought me here had been a happy one. I remembered the sun sparkling on him, his easy laugh as he teased me about the gnomes.

I climbed to the top of the rock and stared at the lake. Its beauty washed over me, but then it was like I couldn't even see it. Dallas's words from our visit here rang in my ears. *I don't have a lot of people in my life who are truthful about what they think and feel.*

I winced. I'd pretended, yesterday. I'd used a script, sullying what we had by not being truthful, by not being brave enough to stand up for myself and what I believed in.

You did it to protect him. But today it seemed a weak excuse.

Maeve whinnied again, startling me out of my wallowing reverie.

"Well, hello there." A figure stepped out from behind the trees.

"Oh!" I scrambled to my feet, heart pounding.

He came closer so that I could finally see him—human, with brown hair and brown eyes. His clothes were dirty and torn.

"I recognize you." His eyes widened. "You're the girl from the palace—the girl I saw with the prince."

Then I remembered him. He was one of the rebel prisoners from the palace, captured during the last attack. I'd seen him in the hallway of the castle.

The prisoner sneered at me. "Who's that? One of the sluts who's here to turn on her own kind and marry the prince?"

Dallas had almost choked him to death, nearly ending him on the spot. But I begged him to stop. By the way the prisoner was looking at me now, I should've let the prince finish.

It was like my tongue had turned to lead. "Y-You're the rebel, the prisoner who escaped."

His dull eyes glittered as he came closer. "That's right."

I looked around, desperate for a stick or a rock, anything I could grab and use to fight him.

"Not so fast, love." He made it to me in a flash, grabbing my wrists and locking them together.

"Get off me!" I struggled, trying to break free.

The prisoner smiled. "I don't think so."

"What do we have here?" Another man came out of the woods. He was young and handsome, dressed in a clean uniform, a far, civilized cry from the fetid rebel who'd captured me.

"A human girl—one from the contest." The prisoner leered at me as I continued to fight.

"Let her go. She doesn't need to be smelling your filth." The other soldier climbed up as the prisoner released me.

He eyed me up and down, as if quickly assessing a use for me. Whatever it was, I wasn't sticking around to find out. I ran for it.

I'd only made it two steps before the young rebel clamped a strong hand around my arm. "You're not going anywhere, except with us." He nodded to the prisoner, who went and grabbed their supplies.

The prisoner took out a rope, bound my wrists, and tied it around me. He took it in his hand like a leash. "We're walking," he explained.

I saw what looked like moss on his teeth. "You might want to find a toothbrush in your pack," I quipped, "or seriously, never talk again."

He got in my face. What I could see of his teeth behind the fuzz of plaque flashed, but the younger rebel pushed him off. "Stay *away* from her. And tell me what you know while we walk."

Maeve whinnied, and they looked at each other. "You have a horse?" the younger man asked.

I didn't answer, deciding from then on that I would not speak to them.

"I say we come back for it later. I saw this one"—the prisoner jerked the rope—"with the prince himself. She was a bit of a pet, I think. Let's get her to the camp. She might be worth something."

"Hmm." The young rebel's face lit up. "You just might be onto something, my friend. Tell me all about it."

CHAPTER 25
THE FACE OF YOU

THERE WERE MORE—MANY MORE—REBELS AT THEIR camp. I winced as I counted. At least twenty men were scattered about. Some of them were sleeping. Some looked at maps. Others played cards. If I couldn't escape Moss-Teeth and Lieutenant Handsome, how on earth was I going to get away from twenty more soldiers?

True to my vow, I'd remained silent, refusing to answer any of their questions. On our long walk to the encampment, the two rebels had seemed to forget about me for the most part, talking as if I weren't there.

"You say you saw her at the castle—explain," the young soldier commanded.

"She was with the prince, just the two of them. I even think they were holding hands." The prisoner warmed to his story, eyes growing larger and voice growing louder. "I said something to her—I said she was a whinging race-traitor—and the prince got all boiled about it. Lifted me up the in the air and almost choked me." He rubbed his neck.

"So why aren't you dead?"

The prisoner jerked his thumb at me. "She called him off, and he listened. I told you, she's his little pet."

"I bet you're regretting *that* decision." The younger soldier smiled at me.

I ignored him.

When we got to the camp, I refused to answer any questions.

"What's your name, sweetheart?" One man asked me.

The soldier next to him peered at me. "How'd you end up out here all by yourself?"

"Those filthy bloodsuckers aren't even taking care of the women they stole from us," another one said. "Letting them wander about like that when there's a war going on... I can't wait to put those monsters in a mass grave."

"Where are you from?" Another rebel asked me.

"She's from Four, I think," the filthy prisoner said. "Ben said he recognized her. Too bad he didn't live long enough to see her like this."

An older rebel peered at me. "What's a nice girl from Four doing hanging around with filthy bloodsuckers, huh?"

I said nothing, head held high. I couldn't believe the rebels—*my people*—were acting like this. They were so filled with hate and prejudice that it had blinded them to any possibility other than their closely held beliefs.

The irony of my situation was not lost on me. I'd been afraid to come to the palace, petrified when I discovered that the members of the royal family were, in fact, vampires. When I started to have feelings for the prince, I worried that I was a traitor to my family. When the prince had slaughtered the human rebels who had attacked the palace, I'd thought him a monster.

But here I was, surrounded by rebels—the same group

my father and brother had joined—and all I wanted was to escape. I silently prayed to get back to the castle in one piece.

But as the hours passed and the sky darkened, that possibility seemed to slip further and further away.

❦

IN MY DREAM, SOMETHING TUGGED AT MY ROPE.

I woke, thrashing. Something *was* tugging at my rope!

"Get off!" But a large, cool hand clapped over my mouth prevented me from screaming. I struggled against my attacker, trying with every ounce of force I possessed to dislodge them.

"Gwyneth. *Gwyneth.*" His voice was so low I could barely make it out. "It's me."

I squinted at the darkness, heart pounding, until Dallas brought his face to mine. "It's me. I'm taking you to safety."

I moaned beneath his hand, eyes swimming with tears. *He'd come for me. Or was this a dream?*

But he loosened the rope quickly, his moves silent and deft. I rubbed my raw wrists. Real, this was real. I tripped and fell against him as I struggled to get up, to free myself from my captivity. Oh, to be a vampire, and not a clumsy human.

But Dallas didn't seem to care that I was only human. He wrapped his arms around me tightly, kissing the top of my head. There was so much emotion between us, I could barely breathe.

But now was not the time. He grabbed my hand and we started to run.

We'd made it to the edge of the camp when I heard it—

some sort of creaking—and then suddenly, a large, heavy web of chains dropped from above.

We were knocked to the ground, captured beneath a chain-link net.

Dallas's skin started to smoke. "Ah!" He cursed, curling up in a ball, trying to get away from the contraption. "It's silver. Try to get it off me," he hissed.

I smelled charred flesh as I struggled to lift the dense net away from him.

Several heavy sets of boots crunched nearby, dropping down from the trees. "Here we are," said a voice in the darkness. *Lieutenant Handsome.* "An excellent haul. Bring the chains," he commanded. "We have ourselves a most-esteemed prisoner."

CHAPTER 26
CAUGHT BETWEEN TWO WORLDS

THEY TIED US UP NEXT TO EACH OTHER BUT NOT CLOSE enough to touch—me in my rope, Dallas in his silver chains.

"Does it hurt? Can you bear it?" I asked.

The prince winced, clearly struggling to compose himself. "It's bearable." But smoke still wafted from his skin where the chains touched him. White tendrils curled into the air then disappeared.

"Are you able to do anything? Use any of your powers?" I kept my voice low. Vampires could talk inside humans' heads, sometimes manipulating them. I'd never seen Dallas do it, but Eve had used it on me a few times. It might help us.

"Not with these." He looked down at his chains.

"I am so sorry." I bit my lip, holding back the tears that threatened. There was no use crying now. Plus, if I started, I might not stop.

"Don't. I should have slaughtered them all before I came for you, but I couldn't bear to leave you tied up and vulnerable like that." Dallas smiled, even though I could tell it pained him. "And I'm the one who got us here in the first place, remember? Stalking off from the stables, all high and mighty."

"You had every reason. I was a fool."

"You're not a fool. You're a young woman who has no experience dealing with the knaves and jesters that populate my world. You're innocent, Gwyneth. It's a miracle and a blessing, and it's one of the things I love about you."

I opened my mouth and then closed it, momentarily stymied.

He laughed, but it sounded strained. "You know, Tariq was probably right. If my father had sent you home, I would've thrown the contest. Perhaps my jester is smarter than I give him credit for."

"Do you think he's smart enough to come looking for us out here?"

"No." Dallas looked down at his chains. "But don't worry. I'll think of something."

The dirty prisoner, who was guarding us, snorted. "You royals are all the same. Think that because you're born with a crown on your head, you've got some special power. I say, take the crown away, and you're nothing, not even a man."

He stepped closer, leering at me, clearly goading Dallas. "Perhaps I should show the young lady what a *real* man's like."

Dallas grinned at him, his teeth large, white, and scary in the darkness. "You know, I'm going to quite enjoy disemboweling you when I get the chance."

"And I'm going to quite enjoy *this* while I have the chance, thank you very much." The prisoner knelt before me.

My stomach lurched as he smiled his fuzzy smile, reaching for me.

"Get the bloody hell away from her!" Another voice rang out. A large soldier with a massive chest stepped forward. He grabbed the prisoner from behind, tossing him out of the way with brute strength. The prisoner landed in a heap, cursing, as the soldier leaned down to peer in my face.

My world went woozy as his brown eyes locked with mine.

"Hey!" called the prisoner from the ground. "What'd you do that for?"

"That's my sister, you ass." Balkyn smiled at me. "And if you ever come near her again, I'll be happy to let the prince disembowel you."

"THEY DIDN'T KNOW. THEY COULDN'T HAVE." BALKYN untied me gently, rubbing my wrists to help the blood-flow return.

"It doesn't matter." I kept my voice low. "It means they would have done it to any of the other girls. The way they've treated me is *not* okay, Balkyn. If you hadn't been here just now..." My gaze traveled over to Moss Mouth. "I don't know what would've happened."

"I'm so sorry. But you're right, and I'll talk to them. You have my word."

"Enough of that." I hugged him fiercely, still not believing my brother was alive and that he'd come to my rescue. "I'm so happy to see you. I didn't know if you were still alive." I wanted to tell him that the prince had been helping me look for him, but I didn't dare.

Dallas hadn't said a word. He watched us silently.

"What're you looking at, bloodsucker?" Balkyn asked him.

"Balkyn."

My brother turned to me. "Don't tell me you're defending this vampire. I know all about that sick contest you've been in. He's had you captive, Gwyn. You've probably got Stockholm Syndrome or some such rubbish."

I took my brother's measure swiftly, and it broke my heart. I didn't risk looking at Dallas.

"I'm fine, I promise, and I'm not defending him." I scoffed. "I just don't think we need to goad him."

I grabbed Balkyn's hand, bringing his attention away from the prince and back to me. "We have so much to talk about. Is father still alive?"

Balkyn's face twisted. "Yes, but he's ill. That's why he's not here."

"What's wrong with him?"

My brother shook his head. "We don't know. He's had a fever for a while, and then for the past few weeks, he hasn't been able to get out of bed."

"Oh no. The poor thing..."

"He'll be all right, I expect. He's a tough one." Balkyn smiled, trying to lighten the mood. "Speaking of tough, how's Mom?"

"She's fine. Winnie and Remy are, too. Winnie just had the flu, but she's better." I refused to look to Dallas, to bring Balkyn's angry attention back to him. *The prince saved her.*

"I'm so glad. You've been getting on without us?"

I shrugged. "Not very well, actually. We've missed you terribly, but we've done our best.

I squeezed his hands. "But...where have you and Father been? I was hoping to have word from you, at some point. It's been so long. We all thought you were dead."

Balkyn's eyes blazed in the darkness. "We couldn't write or come home. We've been...away." His burning gaze flicked to Dallas, and I flinched. "How can we kill this bloodsucker, anyway? Is it true what they say about a stake to the heart?"

"No, actually." I licked my lips. "We just have to wait until the sun comes up."

Balkyn tilted his head, inspecting me. "This one can be out in the sun. I've seen it myself."

I didn't hesitate. "But not for long. If you keep him out all morning, by the time the noon sun hits him, he'll be dead." The lie came forth easily.

I wished I could tell him that silver had no effect. But that proverbial cat was already out of the bag and currently singeing the prince's skin.

"Are you certain?" my brother asked.

"Yes. They can only withstand the sun's rays for so long. In short spurts, some of them are able to move about during the day. Some of them can't tolerate it at all, of course. And the prince can only manage a few hours before weakens so much that he will die."

Balkyn scrubbed a hand over his face. "How do you know all this, sister?"

"They've taught us a lot at the palace with lectures and books. Whoever wins the Pageant will become a vampire's wife. They've been educating us on all the particulars so that we can be prepared."

My brother grinned at me. "Then you are going to come in quite handy."

He stood and reached out a hand for me, pulling me to my feet. "We'll leave the vampire prince till morning then. It'll be dawn soon enough. And when the sun sits highest in the sky, we'll have a toast as we watch him burn."

CHAPTER 27

HOW TO SAVE A LIFE

On Balkyn's arm, I was treated like rebel royalty. My brother bragged that I knew all sorts of vampire secrets, that I would be a tremendous asset to the cause. The men who'd threatened me earlier were now obsequious, offering me ale and blankets.

I thanked them, a smile plastered to my face. But on the inside, I was scheming to get back to Dallas, to somehow get away. I had no idea what I was going to do. Balkyn refused to leave my side. Whether that was because he was thrilled to finally see me again or because he did not trust me, I wasn't sure. I finally fell into a light sleep, propped against a tree, as the rebel men sat around their dying fire.

When I opened my eyes, it was full-on daylight. I struggled to my feet, my heart in my throat.

"Ah, you're awake." Balkyn held out his hand for me. "Come and see."

In the morning light, I could see my brother clearly. He had changed in the years since he'd left home, growing from an adolescent into a man. Always tall, his body had thickened with muscle. His hair, which he'd always worn a bit long, was cut brutally short. And his face was different. Gone were the boyish good looks and cherub cheeks. His cheekbones were more prominent, jutting out of the hard planes of his face, and dark circles ringed his eyes. He looked as if he had suffered greatly. A large scar ran from his ear down the side of his neck, as if something savage had clawed him.

He felt my eyes on him. "I'm sure I'm not as you remembered, but I don't want to talk about it, Gwyn."

"You've been hurt."

He shrugged. "War does that to you."

We walked through the woods in silence for a moment before he continued. "I might not have recognized you, you know. You've changed too. Five years is a long time."

I patted his shoulder. "Too long."

I had mixed emotions about finding my brother, but one still stood out clearly: love.

"I knew you were at the palace for the contest. So when I heard they'd taken a young female prisoner, I had to come see for myself. I had to see if it was you."

I shivered, remembering the filthy prisoner kneeling before me. "I'm so glad you did."

"Me too." He stopped walking. "There's a clearing just ahead. We're keeping the prince there until it's time."

Afraid my voice would betray me, I only nodded in response. We came to the clearing and I tried to keep my face neutral. It was a terrible sight. Dallas sat, chained in silver to a chair, in the middle of a field. Smoke wafted off of him, up toward the sun, which climbed in the sky.

I moved closer and saw marks where the silver had dug into his flesh. *Scorch marks.* I thought I might faint, but

Dallas's gaze flicked to me briefly, giving me strength. I couldn't fall apart. Not now.

"Come and have a seat." Balkyn smiled. He led me a safe distance from Dallas, to the makeshift stands the rebels had erected out of coolers and camping equipment, all the better to watch the prince burn.

The rebels had started another fire. I shakily sat down and watched them. The soldiers laughed and traded stories, drinking steaming coffee from tin cups. One of them flipped bacon in a frying pan he held over the campfire. A picnic. This was a celebration for them.

"I wish father could be here to see this." Balkyn rubbed his hands together as he eyed the prince. He had a sip of coffee then offered me a slice of bacon.

"No thank you." I felt sick, but I sat tall, a fake smile plastered to my face.

There had to be a way out of this. I just had no idea what it was.

꧁ꕥ꧂

THE TIME TICKED BY. THE SUN CLIMBED HIGHER IN the sky.

"Will he burst into flames?" Balkyn eyed the sun's progress.

"I don't think so. I think he just...dies." To my credit, the prince did look weak. He slumped in his chair, head lolled back, smoke rising from his skin.

I wanted to scream. I wanted to run to him and rip the chains off with my teeth, then carry him home. During the time I'd sat around their campfire, I'd noticed that each of the rebels had a gun. Many of them also had large knives strapped into their belts.

Even if I can get one, what on earth am I going to do with it?

"Shouldn't be too long now," Balkyn told the others.

"This is going to be bloody priceless," one soldier said.

"We'll put his head on a spike and bring it to the palace, so he can watch when we slaughter the rest of his family," said another.

I arched an eyebrow at Balkyn. "You're attacking the castle?"

He nodded stiffly. "We've been waiting for the right time.'

"There's not that many of you," I noted.

"We'll figure it out. And now that we have you, you can help us."

Did I imagine it, or was there a testing tone to his voice?

He turned his attention back to the prince, watching and waiting, his hands clenched on his lap.

Don't move, a voice said.

I jerked my head around, startled.

You bloody bootlicking idiot, I said, don't move!

I sat perfectly still. I knew that voice in my head. And I'd never been so glad to hear it.

CHAPTER 28
CRASH TO THE OTHER SHORE

I'M GOING TO GO AFTER THESE MEN, EVE THOUGHT INTO MY head. *Get the silver off the prince, and wait for me there. You won't be able to move him, I don't think. I can't touch him with those chains on him, but he doesn't look good.*

I wanted to tell her about my brother. No matter what had happened, I couldn't sacrifice Balkyn. I couldn't lose him again so soon.

I didn't know what to do. So I didn't move.

What in the bloody hell? I'm not getting any younger, Gwyn!

I hesitated again, but she wouldn't wait. Eve stalked out from behind a copse of white ash. At first glance, she looked pretty and innocent, slim and slight in her pants and tunic, her strawberry-blonde curls glinting in the sunlight. But as she came closer, grinning, her aqua eyes glowed unnaturally, blazing like the sun.

"What sort of demon is this?" one of the rebels shouted.

"One of the fun ones," she said jauntily. Then she showed him her fangs.

I shot to my feet and took off running for the prince.

"Eve!" I shouted, pointing wildly at Balkyn as I ran. "That one's my brother—spare him!"

I didn't look back as I sprinted to Dallas. "Oh, my God." His didn't seem conscious. His eyes were closed, and his jaw was slack.

"Dallas?" I lifted the chains from him. Some had burnt into the layers of his skin, leaving deep, ugly marks behind. Bits of flesh stuck to the chains as I pulled them off as gently as I could. "I am so sorry." Tears spilled down my face, but I ignored them, concentrating on freeing him from the silver. I got the last of the chains off and threw them to the ground, as far away as I could manage.

He sat up suddenly and took a deep, wheezing breath. His eyes snapped open. "Thank you." He turned to me, blinking and dazed. "Are you all right?"

I scoffed. "Are *you*?"

Distracted by the fighting behind me, he didn't answer. I turned, too, afraid for my friend. But Eve was winning. She had a soldier in her grasp, her fangs deep in his neck as he convulsed. The dead bodies piled up around her. The rebels who still lived didn't dare move. She kept picking them off, one by one.

"Do not kill the filthy one—he's mine!" Dallas shouted suddenly, almost knocking me off my feet.

"And do not kill my brother!" I screamed.

I turned back to the prince. "Can you walk?"

"Yes, but probably not that well."

I leaned down, brushing the hair from his forehead and inspecting him more closely. "You didn't answer me before. Are you all right?"

He reached out and stroked my cheek. "I am now."

"I am sorry, Your Dallas." He smiled at my little joke,

and it gave me hope. Even though Eve battled behind us, the words tumbled out. "I did doubt you, when you gave me no reason. It's just that I care for you. Very, very much."

"You don't need to apologize, Gwyneth. You already have my forgiveness. And everything else I have to give." His eyes darkened as he looked past me. "But we should go and help Eve. And...Balkyn."

"Yes." I helped him up out of the chair, but it was a struggle. "Easy. I've got you."

Dallas winced as I placed his arm around my shoulder, and we staggered across the field toward the others. "Let's just take it slow."

Eve dropped another dead rebel to the ground and scowled at us. "I've got this! Stay back!"

"We're coming," I grunted. I sought out Balkyn—he was hunched with the remainder of the rebels. "That's my brother over there. He needs me."

But Balkyn's eyes filled with hate as he watched me help the prince. His face twisted as another rebel fell to Eve.

We finally reached them—what was left of them. Eve had worked quickly.

"Balkyn." I breathed heavily, staggering under Dallas's weight. "I can help you."

"Gwyneth." He took a step back as if I repelled him. "Do not come near me. I can't believe you're a *bloody vampire lover*. This is literally my worst nightmare."

Dallas hissed beside me. I released him gently, stepping between them. "You don't know what you're saying."

Tears filled Balkyn's eyes. "I've given my life to protect you from them. I have given everything to save my family from these beasts."

"It's not like that. Balkyn, *please*."

"I'd rather die than watch you live like this." He took his pistol out, raising it to his head.

"No!" I ran for him.

Eve caught sight of him and closed her eyes. Before I could even reach him, my brother winced, as if he'd been struck. He dropped the gun to the ground and put his hands over his ears. "Get out of my head, witch!"

Eve clenched her fists, concentrating.

"Oh, you bloody beast." Balkyn fell to his knees, his face contorted.

"Eve. *Eve!*"

She opened her eyes, releasing him.

Balkyn stared up at me from the ground, tears on his cheeks. "You have sold your soul to the devil. I don't even know who you are anymore. I only know you are no sister of mine."

My heart twisted. "I'm so sorry that you feel that way. But you're wrong, brother."

Dallas came beside me, a questioning look on his face.

There was only one answer. I reached for his hand.

I would never let it go again.

EVE CLEANED UP AFTER HERSELF EXPEDIENTLY, BUILDING a funeral pyre and burning the bodies immediately. Needing something to occupy myself, I cleaned up the campsite while she worked. Dallas was still weak. He sat quietly on one of the makeshift seats, watching us. Balkyn was tied up nearby. He hadn't said a word. I hoped that, somewhere deep inside, he was deciding to forgive me, and to try to keep an open mind.

"Your Highness," Eve called. She'd finished with the pyre and was holding the escaped prisoner by the scruff of his neck. He squirmed, looking positively petrified.

"What d'you intend to do with this one?" she asked. "I took a whiff of him, and he's quite nasty... But I can eat him if you want me to. I'll just hold my nose."

The prisoner cried out, trying to get away from her.

Eve held him tight. "Oh, do shut up, you wanker."

"Tie him up, and leave him," Dallas instructed. "I will send sentinels to come for him later, and then I'll deal with him when I am feeling more like myself. I have plans for him." The prince's gaze flicked to the prisoner in distaste. "And they're quite intricate."

The prisoner shook with fear. But I didn't feel sorry for him as Eve bound him tightly with rope—the same rope he'd used on me.

Brush your teeth, Moss Man. And next time, don't be so rapey.

But of course, there wouldn't be a next time.

We made a rather motley crew as we dragged ourselves back toward the palace. We collected Dallas's horse then Eve's. Poor Maeve was with them. "There you go. Good girl." I patted her, and she whinnied, scolding me for leaving her behind. I untied her and gently climbed up.

"What were you doing out here, anyway?" I asked Eve.

"His Holiness had finally given me a proper assignment —looking for the escaped prisoner. You're lucky I found you when I did."

"Thank you for saving us."

Eve shrugged. "I told you I was going to help people. Bet your posh little bum didn't think it would need saving, but there you were. And you..." She looked at Dallas and snorted. "That was the sorriest looking thing I've ever seen."

He frowned. "Feel free to keep the ribbing to yourself. I'm still injured."

Eve wrinkled her nose. "How long do the silver's effects last, anyway? I've never seen that before."

"Long enough." His gaze traveled to Balkyn, indicating he'd speak no more on the subject in mixed company.

Dallas rode carefully beside me with Eve taking up the rear. We went very, very slowly. Eve had Balkyn in the saddle in front of her. He didn't dare move, lest she sink her fangs into his neck or start mind-possessing him again.

"So this is your brother?" she asked.

I nodded. "My older brother. Balkyn. I haven't seen him in five years."

Eve appraised him. "Strapping, isn't he?"

"I can hear you, you know." Balkyn sounded irrevocably pissed.

She frowned. "I thought you'd taken a vow of silence. I think I'd like you a bit better if you had."

"Eve. Please."

"Does he know where your father is?" she asked.

"Yes. He said he'd taken ill, though." I thought about it for a moment. My brother might hate me, but we both loved our father. "We can help him, Balkyn. I know you might have some objection to telling me where he is—"

He looked at me with hate. "It's not 'some objection,' Gwyneth. You've joined the other side. You're the enemy. There's no way in hell I'm telling you where our father is."

Dallas frowned, and I knew exactly what he was thinking. There were ways to make my brother talk. I shivered, hoping that we didn't have to use them.

CHAPTER 29
ANOTHER COUNTRY

THE PALACE CAME INTO VIEW. I'D NEVER THOUGHT I'D BE so happy to see it.

"We're going to have to put Balkyn in a cell." Dallas kept his voice low so my brother couldn't hear.

I sighed. "I know. But is it safe? If that other prisoner escaped, I don't know if a lock and key is enough to keep Balkyn behind bars. And I don't want him trying to escape and getting himself killed."

Dallas's nostrils flared. "I'll assign my best guards to monitor him. It's as much for his safety as for ours."

"Thank you, Dallas."

"Don't thank me yet. My father is going to be very hostile about this situation. I'm not sure he'll handle it well."

My heart squeezed. "I understand." But really, I didn't. I had no idea what was going to happen to my brother—or to me.

We reached the stable and Dallas dismounted, slowly,

painfully. A group of sentinels surrounded us in a moment. "Your Highness. What happened?"

"He needs medical attention," I told them. "We were attacked by the rebels. They used silver."

They fussed about, taking his horse and inspecting his wounds until he snapped. "Enough. Take the prisoner from Lady Eve's horse. I want two of you to stay with him until I have a chance to come down to the dungeon. And no harm is to come to him. Do you understand?"

"Yes, Your Highness." Two of the sentinels eased Balkyn down from the horse and dragged him inside.

My heart twisted. "Balkyn—"

"Don't." He wouldn't look at me as they took him away.

I felt as if my heart was shattering, but I didn't let my face betray any emotion. The longer no one knew Balkyn was my brother, the better.

Eve hopped down off her horse. "Well, that was fun." She looked at me. "Are you okay?"

"Yes." *No.* The sight of my brother being dragged toward the dungeons had undone me, not to mention the fact that he hated my vampire-loving guts.

"I'll check on you later. I'll just leave you two to it." She curtsied to the prince and was gone.

"I expect that both of us will have some explaining to do —to the network, the other contestants, my parents..." Dallas offered me a rueful smile. "But all I want to do is change these clothes and lie down."

I looked down at my dress, muddy and torn. "Me too."

"Would you agree to spend a few hours with me...alone?"

"Can we do that?"

"I'm the prince, dammit. And I say yes. Will you join me?"

He reached for my hand, and there was only one answer. I took it.

MY MAIDS WERE NOWHERE TO BE FOUND WHEN I CREPT up to my room. I took the liberty of bathing and dressing myself, grateful for a moment of solitude. After I dressed in a plain black frock and put on zero makeup—which would've given the twins fits—I peered outside my chambers.

The two sentinels Dallas had sent with me stood at attention. "Miss." They both bowed. "His Highness is waiting for you."

I curtsied then quietly followed them down the hall. They brought me up a set of stairs and to the northern portion of the castle where I'd never been before. The royals had their chambers over here. Or so I'd heard.

The guards brought me to an enormous wooden, barn-like door and slid it to the side. I took a deep breath as I walked inside. It was as if I'd entered a different world. On one wall, there was a massive, floor-to-ceiling bookcase, spilling over with books. On another were golden canvases framing oil paintings so vivid, they surely belonged in what they'd called a 'museum' in the old America. A vaulted ceiling and huge windows facing the northern grounds filled the space with air and light. If the chambers weren't big enough to be a whole other world, they were surely big enough to be another country.

And in the middle of the room was a small, rectangular

pool, into which His Royal Highness Prince Dallas Black was dipping his feet.

He'd rolled up his pants to his knees. "My dearest Gwyneth, come and sit." He patted the space next to him.

I kicked off my shoes—a rebellious pair of flats—and went and joined him. I pulled my skirts to my knees and sank my feet into the water. "Oh, it's warm! What *is* this?"

"It's based on what they used to call a 'hot tub' in the old America. It even bubbles."

"Fantastic." I peered at the water.

"Sometimes, when I'm alone, I get all the way in, but I figured that wasn't appropriate for this afternoon."

My cheeks heated. "Good call." Although part of me whined that *it was not a good call at all.*

Dallas chuckled, and I saw that he'd showered and changed. The ugly scorch marks from the silver were still there, but as his overall look had improved.

"Are you feeling any better?"

He shrugged, his movements still stiff. "A bit."

"How long does the pain last?"

"A few days. The marks will fade in time."

I nodded. "That's good."

He smiled. "It is." His face turned serious. "I am very sorry about your brother, Gwyneth. He doesn't seem as though he's going to change his philosophy any time soon. It's a difficult position for you."

"I know. But can you keep him safe?"

"Of course. You have my word." He went quiet for a moment then put his hand over mine. "I haven't told my father yet about your relationship. He knows we have a new rebel prisoner but nothing more."

I sighed. "Thank you for protecting Balkyn. But I imagine you do so at your peril."

Dallas grimaced. "It's not just my peril. I'm worried about you. I must protect you. If the king somehow finds out the truth and I'm not the one to tell him—that's bad for you *and* me."

I nodded.

"But most importantly, I believe in being honest. I've always dealt with my troubles that way. It's better to face these things head on. Then if something bad happens, at least there's one regret I've avoided."

"I understand. We need to tell him."

"We?" He smiled. "I rather like the sound of that, although I'm not sure I want you there when I break the news."

"*We'll* figure it out." I smiled at him. "I rather like the sound of that, too."

"Let me get the last of the un-pleasantries off my chest so that we might enjoy the rest of our time together."

I groaned.

"My guards tell me Tariq's been beside himself because we've been gone."

"I'm sure he's upset."

"It's nothing for you to worry about. I'm meeting with him later, and I'll set him straight. But Gwyneth..." He brushed the hair back from my face. "I have to do what the network says for the remainder of the contest. There's only a bit left. Can you white-knuckle it through to the end?"

"You have saved me, My Lord. You have saved my family more than once. I can do many things, not the least of which is 'white-knuckle it,' as you say, until the contest is done. I don't even know what that means. I only know that

I can, and will, do it." I clasped his hand to mine. "I would do anything for you. Even watch you snog Tamara again."

He chuckled. "There will likely be more snogging. I will attempt to keep it to a minimum, though."

"I appreciate that." I splashed my feet in the tub.

He pulled me against him, resting my head on his broad shoulder. "Are you sure you're quite all right? When that soldier got in your face..."

The muscle in his jaw jumped as he stared at the bubbling water.

"We don't need to talk about that. He can't hurt me. I have you and my brother to thank for that."

He shook his head. "I would have ripped the silver off with my fangs in order to protect you."

I leaned up and kissed his cheek. "I know." *It's one of the things I love about you.*

"The rebels hate us fiercely. They meant what they said about having my head on a spike." Dallas frowned. "I don't want to put you in any more danger."

"The danger is everywhere. But I feel safest with you."

A shadow passed over his face. "But maybe you shouldn't. You never would've been captured if it weren't for me."

"Dallas, don't." I shook my head. "I'm the one who ran off into the forest. And as for whether it's more dangerous with you than without you, I'll take my chances, thank you very much."

He pinched the bridge of his nose. "This is going to be difficult, I'm afraid. Dealing with your brother and your people. They won't accept your choice easily."

"The people who truly love me will. My mother, Winnie and Remy already adore you. My father is a brilliant man. I refuse to believe that he'll shun me. In my heart, I believe that Balkyn'll come around too, eventually."

Dallas tucked me against him and kissed the top of my head. "I hope so."

I snuggled against his chest, careful of his wounds. I inhaled his heady scent. And although my heart still twisted at the thought of Balkyn in the dungeons, the feeling that overwhelmed me was love. Safe, warm, and protected in the prince's arms, all I felt was loved.

I'd read it in a book once, before the war: *Love is another country*.

And in *our* country, there was no hate and there was no prejudice. There was just Dallas and me, in our own happy bubble, the rest of the world and all its troubles miles away.

CHAPTER 30
THE ROYAL GALA

Somehow, the time counting down to the gala passed uneventfully. Tariq avoided me, which suited me just fine. We remaining contestants settled into a dull but comforting routine: breakfast, lessons, lunch, a walk outside, more lessons, dinner. Everything was filmed. Everyone was going on dates except me. We watched the episodes: the contestants giddy with excitement, Dallas tall and handsome and well-mannered. They had him snogging all sorts of girls, of course, including Tamara again.

She crowed about it. She crowed about it a *lot*, and she talked about his juiciness and his handsiness in lurid detail.

I ignored her. I remembered our happy bubble, our own little country. I remembered how Dallas had saved my sister, just as he'd saved me from the rebels.

And I did not doubt him.

Dallas sent me daily updates about my brother. He'd had word that Ballkyn was having a hard time adjusting to prison life. My heart ached for Balkyn, but I stayed away.

He'd been quite clear. He wanted nothing to do with me. So I would fight to keep him alive, but I would also respect what he wanted: to pretend that I didn't exist.

I worried day and night about my father, but at the moment, there was nothing to be done. I wouldn't torture Balkyn into revealing his whereabouts. I prayed that my father had gotten better. I feared, of course, that he had not.

After what had happened with the rebels, I made sure to follow every rule. I kept my head down. I listened to my lessons, counted my fork tines, went to bed early, and ate as many biscuits as I could. Shaye, Blake and I shared every meal together; Tamara graced us with her presence when she wasn't too busy bragging to the other girls about being the front runner.

Finally, the evening of the royal gala arrived.

"This is it," Bria said, pacing my room. "Tonight's the night!"

"I'm ready." In fact, I couldn't wait to wear the beautiful dress they'd selected for me. It was similar to one of the gowns I already had in my closet, but the seamstresses had outdone themselves with the new dress. They'd stitched in intricate details and subtle beadwork that made it one-of-a-kind, a wearable work of art. It was strapless blue chiffon, with shimmering layers that floated around me to the floor. The gown made me look, and feel like, a...princess.

I couldn't wait to wear the dress. I *really* couldn't wait to see the prince.

Bettina hauled out the makeup crate. She had dark circles under her eyes, but an elated smile on her face. "I haven't slept in days. I've been too excited! I'm so glad the gala's tonight."

Evangeline bustled about the room, dusting and straightening things she'd already dusted and straightened three times. "I'm excited too. Are you, miss? I'm sure you'll be happy to see the prince."

I smiled at them, even as Bria forced me into a chair and started attacking the snarls in my hair. "I can't wait. Of course, I'm nervous." I swallowed hard. I'd refused to let myself get too wrapped up in worrying about getting sent home. Now that the gala loomed, my nerves thrummed.

Bria *tsked* above me. "You needn't be worried, miss. We all know you'll make the final four. At the very *least*." She winked at me. "We all believe you'll be the last girl here."

I swallowed over a sudden lump in my throat. "I hope so."

Bettina opened up a container of sparkly highlighter and smiled at me. "You are going to be fine, miss. The prince has liked you since the beginning. The other girls complain that he's very formal with them. They think it's because he only has eyes for you."

"I guess we'll see, huh?"

Evangeline stoked the fire then turned to me. "You don't need to worry. I know it in my heart. We all have a really good feeling about tonight. Don't we, ladies?'

"Yes." Bria smoothed my hair, beaming.

"Absolutely." Bettina patted me on the nose with a fluffy brush.

"Thank you." But as I sat and let them work their magic, I still thrummed with nerves.

Evangeline sensed it. "Oh miss...let me get you some tea. Tea makes everything better."

"O-okay. And Evangeline—thank you. For everything."

She winked as she curtsied, then left the room.

"Now you listen to me." Bria continued to expertly work through my long hair. "You are beautiful, smart, and kind. You are a special snowflake, miss. Don't you let that *Tamara* or anyone else make you doubt it. Not even the little voices inside your head."

"Tell them to sod off," Bettina agreed. She dabbed some more gold glitter onto the brush. "We're here, right next to you, and we think you're wonderful. So listen to us."

I smiled at them. "I am lucky to have you. Not only to help me, but to be my friends."

The twins grinned, obviously touched. "Quite right, miss. Now, let's get you gala-ready." Bria started braiding my hair. "Once we're through with you, I expect that *Tamara* and the little voices inside your head will all take a vow of silence. For good."

⚜

I TOOK A DEEP, STEADYING BREATH AS I HEADED TOWARD the ballroom. I could see the other girls and the camera crews at the end of the hall; it was a mob scene.

I stopped for a moment, resting against the wall. I was excited for tonight, but the nerves were there, thrumming underneath. They threatened to make me a sweaty, disheveled mess.

"Aw, are you nervous?" Blake appeared beside me.

My jaw dropped as I looked her up and down. "Oh my *God*."

She immediately reached for my hand, concern etched into her pretty face. "What's the matter?"

I squeezed her hand. "You are *gorgeous*. My heart almost stopped!"

Blake laughed and swatted me. "Stop. You're the one who's stunning. That dress, wow."

"Yours is so beautiful. I've never seen you in that color before, you look amazing!" It was true. Blake was taller than ever, her thick, blonde hair pulled halfway up, the rest in golden waves hanging over her shoulders. Her dress was lavender, strapless and straight, showing off her curves.

"Well, you can be my date tonight." Blake winked at me. "I'm afraid it's going to be my last here at the palace."

"Don't say that." I linked my arm through hers and we walked toward the queue. Blake was a great friend and a great comfort. I didn't want her to leave the competition. "You said your date went well."

She shot me a look. "We had dinner and then we played basketball. He slapped me five afterward—it was hardly romantic. Besides, you don't really want him to like anyone but you. And I don't begrudge you for it. You have real feelings for him. I have real feelings for biscuits and chocolate tarts." She giggled.

"I don't want him to care for anyone else, it's true." I sighed. "But I want you to stay."

Her eyes glittered. "Whatever happens, I plan to enjoy tonight. I heard it's a *buffet*. Tables heaped with platters, all the food you can bear to eat."

I laughed. Only Blake would be wearing such a dress, about to attend a royal ball, and be solely focused on the food.

Delicious aromas wafted into the hallway and my stomach growled. Maybe Blake wasn't the only one excited about the buffet.

Shaye was ahead of us in line. She scooted back to join us. "You both look lovely." She arranged Blake's hair over her shoulder then squeezed my hand. "Really—you each take my breath away."

I beamed at my friend. "You look beautiful." Shaye wore a dark-emerald gown with gold brocade adorning the front. Her hair was in an elegant twist; she looked positively regal.

"Thank you." She sighed. "I'm quite nervous, actually. I'm not ready to say goodbye. Do you smell that roast?"

Blake closed her eyes and moaned. "We don't have roasts like that in Fifteen."

Shaye scowled. "Or Twenty-Four."

"Don't think about it. Let's just enjoy our night." The three of us linked arms as we waited in line.

Tamara sashayed down the hall, one of the final girls to join the queue, obviously wanting to make a grand entrance. She wore a skintight black mermaid gown. Her enviable assets spilled out of the top as she headed straight for us, cutting the other girls in line. They knew better than to bother protesting.

"Ladies." She looked at our linked arms. "Getting ready to walk the plank together?"

Blake grinned at her and held her arm out. "We're just enjoying the palace and all it has to offer while we can. I might even enjoy hanging out with you tonight. You look quite ravishing, by the way."

Tamara rolled her eyes but accepted Blake's arm. "Of course I do." She didn't say anything for a moment but Blake waited patiently, staring at her. "Oh, you all look pretty too. Are you happy now?"

Blake giggled. "I'll be happy when I stick that roast in my bag and take it back to the slums with me."

Tamara just shook her head. "You and your food."

"A girl's got to eat." Blake turned serious. "A girl's *especially* got to eat while the eating's good, before she gets sent back to her tiny impoverished settlement where there's nothing to do but starve."

The line moved closer to the door and I heard a trumpet, then a sentinel announced the name of the next girl. "Miss Meredith Brisbaine of Settlement Ten."

Tamara's lip curled into a sneer. "Oh that Meredith's a prat. I bet she's going home."

Shaye clutched her stomach. "They're announcing us?"

Blake patted her shoulder. "It's okay. Just stay focused on the buffet."

I tried to stay calm as moved closer. Finally, we could see through the door. Mira Kinney waited on the other side, stunning in a fucshia gown with a Mandarin collar. There were cameras and lights. The ballroom was magnificent, lit with hundreds of candles. It had been decorated with intricately carved Black family royal crests and tapestries in the royal colors, purple, red, and the deepest blue.

Toward the far side of the room, I glimpsed three occupied thrones. "The queen's here?" I whispered.

Tamara pursed her lips. "I hope she already ate."

We were next. Mira beamed at us as we stepped into the room. "Hello girls. Let's take this right to left, shall we?" She leaned over to whisper to the sentinel as the trumpet sounded.

"Miss Shaye Iman, Settlement Twenty-Four."

Shaye smiled as she tentatively stepped forward, into the spotlight. The other girls had formed a receiving line, along with other lords and ladies I didn't recognize. Some of them were clearly vampires.

I leaned over to speak in Blake's ear. "I do hope everyone behaves."

"Nothing's coming between me and that roast." Blake nudged me. "You're up. And His Highness is staring you."

"What? Where?" But the light blinded me. And then the trumpet sounded, and then the sentinel announced me.

"Mis Gwyneth West, Settlement Four."

I remembered Bria and Bettina's ministrations, and Evangeline's barely contained hovering. I thought of Winnie and Remy and Mother. *You can do this.*

I plastered the largest smile I could muster onto my face and stepped out into the spotlight.

I walked forward, smiling at everyone, accepting their congratulations for making it this far in the contest. I nodded and curtsied. I made my way down the line and finally saw Dallas. He was waiting for me, resplendent in his ceremonial uniform.

He bowed deeply. "Gwyneth."

I curtsied. "Dallas."

"You look absolutely stunning." He grinned as he held out his arm for me. "I would like you to meet my parents, again. This seems like more appropriate circumstances."

Since our last meeting had been in the middle of the night, after the prisoner Benjamin Vale had escaped and killed several palace guards, I couldn't agree more. "Okay." I lifted my chin and squared my shoulders. I leaned in close to him. "Do they know about Balkyn?"

Dallas's dark eyes flashed. "Not yet. I'm waiting until after the ball."

That was a relief, but any sense of well-being was short lived as I approached the king and queen. They sat on their thrones, golden crowns atop their heads, and surveyed the gala with sharp eyes that missed nothing. The king was handsome as ever, his shoulders strong and broad beneath his dress uniform. His gray hair and trim, white beard sparkled in the candlelight. The queen was elegant and austere in a silver gown with a high, lace neck. Her sapphire-blue eyes coldly sparkled. Her platinum hair was in an elegant knot at the base of her neck. She nodded toward me and I curtsied, heart pounding in my chest.

"Mother, Father, allow me to introduce Miss Gwyneth West from Settlement Four."

The king frowned. "We have met Miss West before."

"Father." Dallas clasped his hands in front of him. "I know. I want you to meet her again."

The king nodded in my direction. "Miss West."

The queen reached for my hand. I looked at Dallas, unsure, but he nodded. I stepped forward and reached out. She closed her icy hand around mine, and gazed into my eyes. "Eve tells me you're a good friend. I hope that you are a good friend to my son."

"Yes, Your Highness. And he is a good friend to me." She released me and I curtsied again.

Dallas looked at the king, but his father ignored him, watching the crowd instead. "Thank you, Mother." He held out his arm, then whisked me away.

"Are you all right?" I asked.

The muscle in his jaw jumped. "I will be. Gwyneth..." His gaze traveled over me as emotion played out on his face. "I'm sorry my father was so rude. I will speak to him about it."

I smiled, trying to lift his spirits. "No one said this would be easy."

The orchestra started to play and suddenly, the cameras

were upon us. Dallas smiled and held out his hand. "Would you care to dance?"

I took his hand. "I'd love to."

He swirled me around into the center of the ballroom floor. I was not an experienced dancer but Dallas took the lead, his hands firmly guiding me. We danced easily, swaying to the music. The other guests formed a circle around us. The spotlight was there, and Mira Kinney, and Tariq, and all the cameras.

But it all fell away. Dallas smiled at me, and I smiled back. We were in another country, and it was wonderful.

🙒🎜🙑

A TRUE GENTLEMAN, DALLAS DANCED WITH EVERY contestant. Shaye, Blake and I minded the buffet.

"I don't know if I can fit much more into this godforsaken dress," Blake moaned. She eyed a pudding. "But I might have to try."

Shaye giggled. "Did you both enjoy your dances?"

I nodded. "I did. Even with all the cameras and the lights, it was lovely."

Blake frowned. "All he kept talking about was his little brother. He said I'd like him. I don't get it."

Shaye shrugged. "Maybe you'll get picked as a finalist and get to find out."

Blake grabbed the pudding. "I rather doubt it. How was your dance?"

"It was...lovely." She blushed and ducked her head.

"You don't have to be embarrassed." Blake stuck her spoon in the direction of the dance floor. "*She* should be embarrassed. But she won't be."

We turned to find Tamara dancing with the prince, her body in a full-court press against his.

I grabbed a pudding. "Can tonight be over, already? I want to know what happens."

Tariq sidled up next to us, pretending to peruse the desserts. "You've all done well tonight."

"Thank you." Blake and Shaye curtsied.

"We'll see how it goes." I nodded toward him. "Do you know when the finalists will be announced?"

He checked his watch with a flourish. "Oooh, right about now. Put down those desserts, girls. It's show time."

Blake scraped her pudding cup clean before she set it down. She straightened her dress as the song ended and the crowd politely clapped. Tamara was laughing and flaunting her bosom at Dallas.

Mira Kinney stepped forward with her microphone and cleared her throat. "What a lovely couple. Give them another round of applause, everyone." We all clapped and I fake-smiled so hard my face hurt. *This was it.*

"I know we've all become invested in each of these girls and their journeys," Mira continued. "But tonight, as you know, most of them will be going home. We will miss you at the palace, my dears." She clapped and we all joined her.

"The prince has selected four finalists. These are the women he feels the closest to, the ones he believes have the best chance of becoming his wife." A hush fell over the room. My palms started to sweat. "The final four contestants will remain at the palace for one last week with the royal family. The prince will visit each of their settlements and meet each girl's family. At the end of that week, the winner of the Pageant will be announced. And then, the planning for the royal wedding will begin."

Mira beamed at us. "Now please give a warm reception to His Royal Highness, Prince Dallas Black, Crown Prince of The United Settlements."

The crowd erupted into cheers. But as Dallas strode forward and took the microphone, quiet descended. No one wanted to miss a word from His Highness's mouth.

"Good evening, and thank you all so much for being here. My father and mother join me in gratitude for each of you sacrificing time away from your families and homes to join us here. This show of solidarity means everything to us." He smiled as the cameras circled him, bathing him in klieg lights. "Sadly, for some of you, your time at the palace has come to an end. If I could, I would keep each of you here. Instead, you will be sent home tonight with your stipends."

There was more polite clapping before the prince continued. "Each contestant has a story and background that make you unique and very special to me. I've enjoyed our time together so much. But now I have to narrow the contestants down. I want you to know I did not undertake this choice lightly. One of the four finalists will become my wife, and I will choose her for love, for the good of the people, and for the hope of the brightest future. Each of you are a wonderful person, an amazing young lady. I hope that you all enjoy a long and happy life, and I'm so thankful that you got to be part of mine."

He blew out deep breath. "I will now call the four finalists. I will ask each of them if they would like to remain in the competition. It's a bit unnerving, actually."

Everyone chuckled politely and Dallas cleared his throat. "Miss Shaye Iman, from Settlement Twenty-Four."

Shaye looked at us, wide-eyed, and Blake and I nodded at her. She stepped forward, toward the prince. He held out his hand for her. "Miss Iman, will you accept my invitation to stay as a finalist?"

Shaye curtsied, then nodded. "I will."

Tariq collected her and brought her to the side.

"Blake Kensington, from Settlement Fifteen."

Blake's jaw dropped. "Oh bloody hell. I think I have pudding in my teeth." Still, she strode to meet Dallas and curtsied.

The prince grinned at her. "Miss Kensington, will you accept my invitation to stay as a finalist?"

Blake grinned back. "Absolutely." Tariq assembled her next to Shaye, then nodded for Dallas to continue.

"Miss Tamara Layne, from Settlement Eleven."

Tamara strutted slowly to the prince, making sure the camera got a good, long look at her. She curtsied deeply, somehow making it look sensuous.

"Miss Layne, will you accept my invitation to stay as a finalist?"

"Yes, Your Highness." She eye-snogged him as Tariq led her next to the other girls.

My palms were slick with sweat. Blood rushed in my ears. *One finalist left.* And if it wasn't me? What on earth would I do then?

"Miss Gwyneth West, from Settlement Four."

I sighed deeply and went to Dallas. He smiled at me, all kindness and goodness and strength. And even though Tamara glared, the king looked on disapprovingly, and the klieg lights threatened to singe us both, I suddenly felt calm.

Dallas beamed at me. "Miss West, will you accept my invitation to stay as a finalist?"

There was only one answer. I reached for his hand. "Yes."

AFTERWORD

Thank you so much for reading this book! It means everything to me! The next book is coming soon!

If you enjoyed *The Gala*, **please** consider leaving a review here: Amazon-The Gala. **Short or long, reviews help other readers find books they'll enjoy. It doesn't have to be fancy—just a quick few words that you enjoyed the book!**

This is a brand-new series, so your review means a lot! Thank you so much for considering it!

The next book is coming soon! You can subscribe to my newsletter for new-release notifications:

https://www.leighwalkerbooks.com/subscribe.

Thank you again. It is THRILLING for me to have you read my book. Please sign up for my newsletter and come along for Dallas and Gwyneth's exciting adventures!

xxoo

Leigh Walker

ABOUT THE AUTHOR

Leigh Walker lives in New Hampshire with her husband and three adorable, brilliant, talented children who play almost every sport on the planet and only help clean the house when direct threats are issued.

In her pre-author life, Leigh had many different jobs. She worked in advertising at *Boston Magazine* and was a copy editor at *Chadwick's*, the women' fashion catalog. She was also a barback, waitress, barista, receptionist and lawyer. She loves being a full-time writer and sports-mom best.

Outside of writing and family, her priorities include kindness, maintaining a sense of humor, caffeine, chocolate, Grey's Anatomy, Jessica Jones, and Chris Rock's "Tamborine."

She loves to hear from readers! Email her at leigh@leigh-walkerbooks.com, and sign up for her mailing list at www.leighwalkerbooks.com.

www.leighwalkerbooks.com
leigh@leighwalkerbooks.com

ACKNOWLEDGMENTS

Thank you to my readers for joining me! Your support means everything. Readers for the win!

I must give credit to the writer James Baldwin, author of *Another Country*, from which I took the quote: "Love is another country." Yeah, it is. The loveliest country of them all.

Speaking of love, I must give love to my family, who puts up with my blank stares, my crazy ideas, and me in general. A special shout out to my kids, who endured me on multiple snow days while I was writing this book. Love, love, love you. Love for the win!

Thanks to my mom, who always supports and helps me. Moms for the win!

I also want to thank my editors at Red Adept Editing. They edit all my independently published books, and I love working with them. They're the best. It's so nice to have a team, even when I'm a free agent!

The next book is coming soon! I can't wait to share it with you!

That's a lot of exclamation points in a few short paragraphs, lol. But this book world gets me excited, and so does the fact that you're coming along for the ride. I'm signing off to write now, but just so you know, I am, forever and truly, **#teamdallas.**

See you in the next book!

xoxo

Leigh

PS: Sign up for my mailing list at www.leighwalkerbooks.com so you know when the next book comes out!

CPSIA information can be obtained
at www.ICGtesting.com
Printed in the USA
LVHW051532070519
616953LV00001B/83/P

9 781980 955559